RAVEN ROCK

RAVEN ROCK

A Novel of Suspense

Mignon F. Ballard

DODD, MEAD & COMPANY
New York

First Edition
3   4   5   6   7   8   9   10

Library of Congress Cataloging-in-Publication Data

Ballard, Mignon Franklin.
Raven rock.

I. Title.
PS3552.A466R3   1986   813'.54   85-25349
ISBN 0-396-08794-9

For Melissa and Amy

RAVEN ROCK

One

I knew I had found the town the minute I saw it. It was no prettier and no uglier than many other towns its size. But it was right. The trees were the right green. The sky was the right blue. The shaded streets were polka-dotted with sunshine. How could anyone be afraid here?

A familiar sense of warning, like a gentle hand on my shoulder, came and was gone, so quickly I thought I must have imagined it. But I knew I hadn't. It had happened too many times before, and never without reason. I would have to be careful here.

Raven Rock was just another mountain town, I told myself. I had no reason to believe my mother had ever walked these streets, climbed these hills, waded knee-deep in the asters that lined the fields.

My mother, Maggie Grey. The unfamiliar words sucked the breath from me, left me gasping, as they had when I had first heard them two months before.

I drove slowly past the faded red-brick courthouse with its towering clock face watching through the trees; past the postage-stamp park where a statue of a confederate soldier stared thirstily as sprinklers played among the marigolds in the late August heat. Few people were on the streets. It was after five o'clock, and the shops in the tiny business district would be closing for the day.

The man at the gas station had said there was a motel on the other side of town, the lake side he had said. As I wound my way through the narrow lanes of homeward bound traffic, I felt a sense of loneliness, an urgent need to belong. I glanced at the motorist in the lane beside me, a neat, middle-aged woman with a sack of groceries on the seat next to her.

Is that you, Mother? I thought. Is that you, Maggie Grey, rushing home to cook supper for your family? What about the one you abandoned? What about me?

The woman returned my stare with a puzzled smile, and I forced myself to nod, pulling ahead of her in a swoop of speed. I was disgusted with my infantile fantasizing, disgusted with myself. I needed time; time to rest, to think; time to work things out with myself.

The lake almost blinded me when I came upon it, a golden echo of the sun. Then the road curved away to the other side of the mountain and the Raven Rock Motel.

It was clean and simple, and certainly not over-crowded. Mine was only the sixth car there. The desk clerk didn't seem to think I was going off the deep end when I asked her about the biking trails. Since it was only five-thirty when I checked in, there would be several hours of daylight. Although I had brought my bike along with me, I hadn't had a chance to use it in weeks. I was almost like a child in my eagerness.

The clerk reached for my key on a peg behind her. "Oh yes, there's a lovely trail around the lake. I expect you'll want to see the rock." She handed me the key with a smile. "That's where the town gets its name, you know."

"The rock?"

"Raven Rock. It's a great, huge, black boulder right at the head of the falls." She stretched her arms to encompass the small lobby. "Shaped just like a bird! You can't miss it. There are plenty of back roads around here too," she added, "if you mind the traffic."

I thanked her and hurriedly tossed my belongings into my room, only taking time to change into jeans and a T-shirt. Tomorrow I would be the dignified young lady. Tomorrow I would look for my mother, and maybe a job. But today, with a fried chicken picnic boxed obligingly by the motel restaurant, I was going to explore Raven Rock.

I felt light-headed as the pedals whirled under my feet, as if I had no body at all. I had almost become accustomed to these flights of fancy. They had been occurring more and more often since the beginning of the summer, when I had discovered that I was not who I thought I was.

My life had always been planned for me, boring, maybe, but secure. I had been raised by loving, middle-aged parents, who tended to shelter me more than a younger couple might. My father had owned and managed The Sugarplum, a successful bakery, and after his death during my junior year in high school, the business passed to my mother and me. A few short months ago I had a home, a devoted mother, and a promising career ahead of me. Now I didn't even have a name.

My front tire hit a stone in the road, jarring me out of my daze. I had decided to explore one of the winding rural roads before having my supper at the lake. Now the smell of the chicken, still warm in its box in my basket, made me look around for a place to eat. The drying cornfields on either side offered no shade, and the bull in the pasture ahead, no encouragement, so I decided to live with my hunger a while longer.

I watched the dusty blur of the road beneath my wheels and felt the ache in the calves of my legs that comes from biking. But it was a good kind of ache that meant my muscles were adjusting to the exercise. It meant that I was a real person. Only real people feel pain and hunger. For a while I had not been conscious of these things. Bit by bit, I was coming back to life.

The hard rubber bar grips were warm and smooth beneath my fingers. It felt right to touch something familiar and know it was a part of my life, like an old friend. Four years before, a girl named Henrietta Meredith had received the bike as a gift from her mother before starting college. Now there was no mother; there was no Henrietta Meredith. But the bike was the same.

I had noticed that my mother was becoming frail during my senior year at the university, but she blamed it on a bout with the flu and long hours at the bakery. I spent my spring vacation working in the shop, and Mom had promised me then that she would see a doctor about her weight loss.

She had called me just before graduation to tell me that she was going in the hospital for a checkup but would be out in time to see me receive my degree in journalism.

She didn't come. Emmett Lieberman came instead. Emmett, Mom's partner and head baker at the store, was the closest friend my mother and I had. I couldn't remember when he hadn't been with us. I waited in the hot stadium after the ceremony, diploma in hand, searching for my mother's face in the host of people

4

swarming onto the field. My classmates were seized up in a whirlwind of handshakes, hugging, and laughter, leaving me a lonely island in their midst. Then I saw Emmett, alone, and I knew there had been more to my mother's hospital visit than a routine checkup. She had waited too long for this day.

"She asked me to come in her place, Henri, and to bring you home. She's waiting to see you." Emmett wrapped me in his kind, husky arms, and my tears overflowed on his only good suit, which he never wore to the bakery but which somehow smelled of strudel. His words were choked. "She wanted to come. She would have, you know."

I knew. And I knew when I saw the sallow shell of my mother on the white hospital bed that I wouldn't have that part of her much longer. All she had left was love; it was there in her eyes, in her face. And she needed love as well as strength to tell me what she had to say. How difficult it must have been for her to say those words, words that would leave the world spinning one way and me another. I could see that she was struggling with herself, fighting for self-control. I kissed her forehead, stroking away a strand of soft, gray hair. The proper smell of florist's carnations and hospital linen sickened me. I wanted to run, to hide until this nightmare went away.

"Henri," Mom whispered, forcing her eyes to meet mine. "My own little Henrietta, you'll always be mine, always . . . but I'm not your mother."

Two

"I'm not your mother." It's funny how those words affect me, even now, especially now that their meaning has had time to soak into my very being.

Panting, I pushed the bike to the top of a hill where I rested gratefully on a large gray rock by the roadside. A cool breeze lifted my damp hair, and for a minute I shivered, but the rock was warm against my back, and the sun still simmered in the sky. I could see the main road below, and farther on a steellike sliver of water winked through the trees.

You are here, I thought. It was almost like an echo in my head. It was strange that I should feel so peaceful in this place, so right. Maggie Grey had not felt right, Mom had said. Nor had she felt peaceful. "She was afraid of something, deathly afraid," Mom had told me. And she had left her baby daughter with the Merediths, never to return.

She was an enigma, this Maggie Grey, this woman who had been my mother. Mom had smiled a little as she told me about her that night just a few days before she died. Emmett was there too, to lend support to both of us, Emmett who had known my story all along.

"She came to us looking for work," Mom began. "She must have been about your age, Henri, maybe a little older, and so very frail and tiny! She had just lost her husband, she said. She told us she liked to cook, so we gave her a job in the kitchen." She smiled at Emmett. "We always need help in there. But when it became obvious that the girl was pregnant, we moved her up front as a clerk." Mom looked to Emmett for encouragement.

"She was a bright little thing, Maggie was, seemed educated, too. And she got on well with the customers. They liked her. We all did," Emmett added softly. "She never said much, but she didn't have to. She was just one of those people—you knew she was okay."

"Your dad and I took her in to live with us," Mom said. "She'd been staying in a cheap rooming house. She didn't know anyone, and we had all that room to ourselves. We were fond of Maggie. There was a quality about her, a goodness . . . oh, I know that word's not popular today!" A little strength came back into her voice. "You have it too, Henri, and you look a little like her. You're slender as she was, but taller. And her hair was darker, a chestnut brown almost. Her eyes were brown too; yours are more of a hazel. There's a picture of her at home, a snapshot. I saved it for you."

I tried to speak calmly, as if it didn't really matter. "But her husband, my father, what . . . ?"

Mom shook her head. "There was no husband. Never was. She admitted that later. We never learned who your father was or anything about him. Maggie kept things to herself, never said where she came from. And if she had any relatives, we didn't know about them. She wanted it that way."

Emmett frowned. "I remember once, just before you were born, Henri, I asked her if she didn't want us to get in touch with her family. 'You're my family,' she told me. 'You and the Merediths, you're all the family I have.' "

"Once or twice she let things slip," Mom added. "Maybe it was deliberate, but I don't think so. I think she was homesick, poor little thing. It was in the fall when the leaves were beginning to turn. She said something about the mountains, how much more colorful they were." Mom closed her eyes. "I think she mentioned the North Carolina mountains, but I'm not sure." She sighed. "Then another time we were eating in one of those restaurants that specializes in seafood, and Maggie told us about a lake somewhere in the mountains that was so clear you could see the fish on the bottom. She said they used to catch the trout and cook them over a campfire by the lake. She said it like they did this a lot, Henri. That's why I think that's where she lived, somewhere in the mountains of North Carolina, somewhere near a lake."

Mom stroked my cheek with her fingers. "I know we should have tried to find out more about her, Henri, but we were selfish. We were content with the way things were. And after you were born, well, both of you became a part of our family. It seemed like things were working out for all of us until Maggie—" She turned to Emmett. "If we had only known what frightened her so! Maybe we could have done something, maybe we could have helped."

I frowned. "Frightened? Why?"

Mom nodded. "We never knew why, but the fear grew in her day by day, almost like a disease."

"Do you think it was because of me?" I asked. "Could someone have been threatening her? Blackmailing her because she was pregnant?"

Mom shook her head. "I thought about that. No, I don't think so. It was more than that. She was terrified! It got to be an obsession with her. We were afraid she was losing her mind."

"It seemed to begin in little ways," Emmett noted. "She jumped every time a customer walked in, nervous as a cat, like she was afraid someone would recognize her."

"So, we let her handle the clerical work in that little office partition, billing and filing, things like that. She could hide back there." Mom accepted a sip of water and allowed me to slip another pillow behind her. "And the telephone! If the phone rang at home, she refused to answer it. Said she'd had some crank calls."

I leaned forward. "Did she tell you any more?"

"One time she said she believed her life was in danger. I honestly didn't know whether to believe her or not. You see, at first it wasn't as noticeable. We thought it was probably because of her situation. But as the time drew nearer for the baby to be born, she kept more to herself, wouldn't even leave the house except to go to the doctor. And the locks! She made your dad install extra locks on all the doors. It was like living in a jail!"

I turned to Emmett. "Do you think she was insane?" His opinion was important to me. I had to know.

"Her terror was real, Henrietta. But Maggie was a practical person, not at all the emotional type this might lead you to believe. Of course, she was going through a trying period at the time, but she seemed to be adjusting well until . . ." Emmett rubbed both hands over his red-rimmed eyes. "Oh, just a few months

9

before you were born. Then we couldn't even reason with her."

"We thought she might improve after the baby came," Mom said. "But she didn't. If anything, she was worse."

I walked to the window, watched the soft June shadows seep into the parking lot below. My eyes felt as if they were made of burning glass.

Mom stirred in the narrow bed. "Not long after you were born, a letter came for Maggie. She read it in her room, read it over and over, I suppose. She stayed in there for hours. The next day she told us she had to leave, that there was something she had to do."

My voice sounded miles away. "Was it the letter? Something in the letter?"

Mom nodded. "I think so, but we never saw it. It was the only mail she received the whole time she was with us. It had something to do with her decision, I know that."

"She didn't say where she was going?" I was hoping against hope.

"She only said she was going back," Mom answered. "And, Henri, she made us promise to take care of you. 'If anything happens,' she said, 'if I don't come back, promise me you'll take care of my baby. Promise me you'll love her as I do.'"

"But what happened to her? Where did she go? Why didn't she come back?" I could no longer keep the pain out of my voice.

Mom's gentle voice soothed me, as it had so many times before. "Henri, darling, I don't know what was troubling your mother. But I know one thing: If she could have come back, nothing could have kept her

10

away. Your dad and I loved you, Henri. I don't think I have to tell you that. You were our own little girl, as surely as if you had been born to us. But Maggie Grey loved you first."

Three

Did she? Thoughtfully, I rubbed my tingling leg, which was protesting its cramped position on the rock. Did my mother leave me because she was in danger, or did she conveniently dump an unwanted baby on a middle-aged, childless couple? I had to find out.

A car, carrying a canoe on top, approached from the direction of the lake, stirring the thick dust as it went by. Fishing poles jutted from the windows. I wondered if you could see the fish at the bottom of Raven Rock Lake.

The shadows were longer as I crawled from my granite perch, and my appetite told me it was past my usual dinner hour. I looked at my watch and was surprised to find it was after seven. It was good to be hungry again!

During those dreadful days before Mom died and the weeks that followed, I had had to force myself to eat, spurning even the tempting pastries Emmett offered from the bakery.

Emmett had been my anchor in those leaden days, patiently explaining in his kind, gruff way the things that Mom had neglected to tell me.

"Your parents should have had ten kids," he told me during one of our vigils at the hospital. "But they waited too long to apply for adoption. They were in their early forties then; they were too old." He smiled. "You must have been an answer to their prayers, you and Maggie. She was like a daughter to them, too." Emmett shook his head. "All that waiting after she went away, it almost tore them up. But they waited. They waited and waited for Maggie Grey."

We were sipping a sustaining cup of coffee in a small restaurant near the hospital. I stirred mine absently. "Didn't they even try to find her, Emmett? Didn't they look at all?"

Emmett glared at me as if I had just been caught with my finger in one of his meringues. "And where would they have looked? Your mother never told them where she was going, wouldn't even let us drive her to the bus—if she took a bus. We didn't want her to leave, Henri, none of us did. Remember that!"

I felt as if I had had my hand slapped. The coffee was bitter, but I drank it anyway, as a sort of penance. I must have looked contrite, because Emmett patted my arm with his big hand. "I shouldn't have nipped at you that way."

I grinned. "Nipped? You mean devoured, don't you?"

"Listen, Henri," he said, "Maggie Grey didn't want us to find her. She told us that, and we had no idea where she went. She asked your dad to drop her off downtown on his way to the shop. After that I suppose she called a cab. No one remembers seeing her in the bus station or the depot." He poured another inch of sugar in his cup. "Maggie told us she would be back in a few days. The Merediths waited six months to take steps to adopt you, and, since your legal mother

13

had left you in their care willingly, this time they were approved."

"I wonder if I have relatives," I said as we walked back to the hospital. "There has to be somebody somewhere."

"Dreaming up a rich uncle?" Emmett smiled. "I'm not rich, but I'm available."

I linked my arm through his. "Silly! You know what I mean."

He nodded. "Of course you're curious. Who wouldn't be? I expect you do have relatives somewhere. Your mom and dad never tried to find them, and for good reasons. They were afraid they might lose you if they did. And also Maggie had really frightened them, I think, about the danger she was in. Fear is contagious, you know, real or imagined."

My mother died that next evening but she was conscious almost to the end. I like to think that she died peacefully, as she had lived.

"You won't hold this against me, will you, Henri?" she had asked that last morning. "You won't love me less?"

I had been brushing her thinning hair. I dropped the brush on the bed and put my arms around her.

"I should have told you all this before," she said against my face. "I know that. But I was afraid you might try to find her. And Henri, she's not here. Your mother's gone. I know it." She relaxed against the pillows. "Remember how we used to joke about your guardian angel?" There was a glimmer of a smile in her eyes. "Remember the day you missed the school bus and there was an accident, some of the children were hurt? And the night you made us all change our seats at the ball game just before the bleachers collapsed? There were other times, too. Well, I believe you really do have a guardian angel, Henrietta, and I think you know who it is."

"Promise me one thing," she murmured just before closing her eyes. "I know you, Henri, and I know you're going to want to look for your mother. Don't. Please don't. You have your whole life ahead of you. Don't look back."

A few days after the funeral I went through the house, noting the things I wanted to keep. It was empty and musty, a shell of the home it had been. I hurried through my grim task, shutting the door on that part of my life forever. It was the most painful day of my life.

My mother's personal belongings, except for a few cherished keepsakes, went to the Salvation Army. It was what she had wanted. Emmett agreed to store the few good pieces of furniture in a room over the bakery. I sold the rest and turned the house over to a realtor. I also made arrangements for Emmett to buy the business, as it was always understood that he would assume full ownership when Mom retired.

With the money from the sale of the furniture, I bought a small car. And that, with my bike and a few personal belongings, was all I took with me in my search for Maggie Grey. All I had that had belonged to my mother was a yellowed snapshot and the book of poetry in which it had been found. The picture was just where Mom had said it would be, in a book of Emily Dickinson's poems that had been concealed beneath some papers in the false drawer of her desk. Maggie Grey had taken most of her things with her when she left. But this, which must have been a favorite volume, had slipped between the bed and the wall. A faded inscription on the fly leaf read: "To Maggie with love, C." I had come up with several versions of who

"C" might be, from Charlie to Charlene. From the worn appearance of the book, it had been read a lot during the short time she had it, which led me to believe that Maggie Grey thought highly of Emily Dickinson, or "C," or both!

The photograph showed a group of five women posing in front of a large Victorian house. Emmett pointed out the one who was my mother. I would never have picked her for mine. She was beautiful! The black-and-white snapshot was a small one and at least twenty-three years old, but I could see that she was lovely. Her short, dark hair fell in careless waves about a small, delicate face. Bright, round eyes laughed at the camera across the shoulder of a friend who was clowning at the photographer. They were wearing the clothes of twenty-odd years ago. If it had been someone else's photograph, it would have been funny. But it wasn't funny. It was all I had.

I reached to touch the snapshot in my shirt pocket as I pedaled toward the lake. I kept it with me always. Except for the book of poems, it was the only physical link I had with my natural mother, the only thing I could touch. It was still there, safely buttoned next to my breast, and I, like the fool I was, felt reassured that all was well.

I had a feeling of isolation as I turned onto the lake road. I knew there must be other people there, but I didn't see them. There had been sun on the main road, but here in the shade it was twilight, and quiet. The silence was like a tranquilizer, and I stopped for a while by the side of the lake so I wouldn't spoil it. The water varied in color from brown to a clear green and probably was very deep in spots. I closed my eyes, smelled the earthy, summer smell of water and sun and dusty grass, and jumped as a fish splashed and the wind stirred the bushes behind me.

Munching on a cold chicken leg, I wound lazily around the lake, passing several people fishing from a pier and a party of teenagers who were throwing each other from a raft. They weren't a lot younger than I was, but I felt old enough to be their grandmother. I was relieved to find I was not alone, but I didn't enjoy the thought of eating my lunch by myself in the presence of others. I decided to bike to the far end of the lake and look for a spot away from the crowd. As I rode nearer, I could see a silver spray of water tumbling into the lake from a craggy height and shivered at its cold, crystal call. Then, as the trees thinned momentarily, I saw for the first time where the town got its name. The rock *was* like a raven: large, dark, and menacing. Edgar Allan Poe would have loved it. I didn't. I hurried down the trail to find a place to eat my solitary meal. The image of the rock overwhelmed me. Even when I tried to turn away, it demanded my attention, looming there at the top of the falls like an evil omen.

Four

A narrow, scraggly path branched off the main trail. I wheeled the bike over its serrated surface, glad to be turning away from that rock, lured by the uncertainty of the way ahead. A giant oak nodded invitingly from the other side of a hill; it looked as if it had been there forever. A cool, peaceful dining nook for a tired cyclist, its huge branches beckoned a welcome.

Finding it impossible to ride through the tall grass, I concealed my bike in some pine seedlings and continued on foot, lunch in hand. The bubblings of a small mountain stream competed in volume with the rumblings in my stomach, which was indignant at having been denied supper. The stream, which had been hidden from my view by a stand of young oaks, was neither as shallow nor as small as I had expected, and the only means of crossing it was by way of a moldering foot log. I looked at the tree, at its deep green shade; I looked at the dusty trail and the thigh-high weeds where chiggers and ants licked their chops over my vulnerable hide. They probably hadn't had dinner yet either! I prodded the log with one toe. It shook slightly but nothing crumbled. I stepped on the end; it shivered and was still. So was I. Breathing softly, so as not to disturb my perch, I surveyed the way ahead. It was a large, sturdy-looking log, probably from one of the huge oak's late brothers. I told myself that it had been there for years and would probably be there for many more. That's what I told myself.

The ancient, moss-filled furrows were like a carpet to my sneakered feet as I inched to the middle of the stream. Arms outstretched, I grinned triumphantly, remembering how long it had been since I had indulged in such stunts. But my confident smile vanished as with a terrifying creak the massive limb split in slow motion.

Strangely, all I could think of at the time was saving the lunch, which I hurled with abandon at the opposite bank as I slid shrieking into the water.

The water was cold, as I had expected, and I was shaken, shivering, and not at all pleased with the situation. The icy water slapped against my waist as I sat spraddled on the squishy bottom of the creek, and I sensed for the first time the sharp stone etching its image in the palm of my hand.

I splashed to my feet, watching miserably as my sodden box of chicken gurgled to the bottom of the stream. Shivering, I teetered on mossy stones, hugging myself to keep warm. And it was beginning to look as if I might make it, when a leafy pole appeared from nowhere and nudged me back into the water!

"Hey, watch it!" I spewed out a mouthful of gritty water.

"I'm only trying to help. Grab the pole, and I'll pull you out." A head materialized through the foliage on the bank; then an arm appeared, waving a threatening stick. It didn't seem to have a body.

"Are you hurt?" A man stepped out, a rugged, rangy, cross-looking man.

"I'm too cold to tell," I said, oozing back into the mire. (I was beginning to feel at home there.) "Thanks, but I think I can manage. It doesn't look as steep here." Ignoring his offer of help, I sloshed to the bank.

He shrugged, tossing the stick aside. "Suit yourself, but if you'd stay off private property, you wouldn't be in this mess. Didn't you see the sign?"

Hanging on to a root on the creek bank, I inched my way up the slope. "What sign?" I clenched my teeth to keep from chattering.

He stood with folded arms, watching my progress. He was tall, dry, and grinning, and I hated him. "The 'No Trespassing' sign on the lake road. I'm sorry about your accident here, but this isn't public property."

"Sorry," I said, in a voice that was cool enough to match my body temperature. "I must have missed it." I drew myself up to a waterlogged five feet, five and a half inches. "Look, I had no intention of vandalizing your property. It looked like a likely spot for a picnic, and I was hungry."

For a minute he looked embarrassed, even regretful, but it didn't last long. "Well, there was a sign, but hardly anyone uses that path anymore. It could have fallen over."

I sniffed, really seeing him for the first time. He wasn't a bad-looking man, but I noticed that his ears stuck out.

His cool, green eyes swept over me. "You'll need to get out of those wet clothes. I think I can find something up at the cabin." His words were reluctant, as if he had to prize them out with a crowbar.

"That's all right, my bike's on the other side of the creek," I explained. "If you'll just show me how to get back over there, I'll be on my way." And the sooner the better, I thought. I knew that raven had been an omen.

One side of his mouth turned up in what was meant to be a grin. "Not like that, you won't," he said, eyeing my wet T-shirt. "You might get picked up for indecent exposure."

I glanced at my shirt front, which clung to my body in revealing wetness. My shirt was white and thin; my bra was also white and thin. Both were transparent with water. I looked up. He was smiling broadly now. I sneezed.

"Come on before you freeze to death." He turned and started up the path, not waiting for me to follow. I squished in his footsteps, hugging myself for modesty's sake.

We walked the remaining yards to the cabin in silence. There I was provided with a hot shower, dry clothes, and more silence. The shower was pure luxury, even if I did have to wash my hair with deodorant soap. And the clothes were presentable: girl's jeans and a plaid shirt, which more or less fit. I was getting used to the silence.

I emerged from the tiny bedroom to find my host lighting a fire in the enormous stone fireplace. "It's a little early in the year, but it gets cool here at night." He appraised me with his cool stare, and I had a feeling I came up lacking. "It will give you a chance to dry your hair."

I moved closer to the warmth as my shaggy brown pageboy dripped onto my shoulders. "I hate to leave a good fire," I said, "but I do have to get back. If you'll just show me where I can find my bike . . ."

He stood abruptly and wiped sooty hands on his jeans. "Don't be ridiculous! It's almost dark. I'll drive you and your bike to town, but I'll not be responsible

21

for your getting pneumonia." He moved to an adjoining kitchen and returned with a steaming pan. "Besides, I know you're starving. I saw your lunch go down for the third time." He dumped the contents of the pan into a waiting bowl. It smelled delicious. "Eat," he commanded.

It was canned stew, but it was hot and it was filling. The stew was served with soda crackers, slightly stale, and coffee that must have been brewed in heaven.

"Forgive me for not joining you in your meal." My host straddled a chair opposite mine. "But I ate earlier; rude of me, but I wasn't expecting company."

My face felt warm, and it was not from the fire. "You make excellent coffee," I said, lifting my mug in a salute. "Is it a special recipe or do you chant something over the pot?"

He laughed. "Touché! I promise not to turn you into a toad if you won't give me away." He poured us both another scalding cup, which I couldn't refuse. "I'm Morgan Lawrence, local warlock and reluctant rescuer of drowning maidens."

"Henrietta Meredith," I replied. "And I really wasn't drowning, I . . ."

He lifted an eyebrow. "And you're not a maiden?"

I stared at him over the rim of my cup just long enough for the silence to soak in. That kind of question didn't deserve an answer.

"You needn't worry," he said, whipping away my empty bowl. "I won't attempt to alter the situation."

I heard him in the kitchen rinsing my bowl and spoon and felt a pang of conscience for not offering to help, but it was a minor pang and I stayed where I was, sipping my coffee and admiring the room.

If the circumstances had been different, I could have appreciated the rustic beauty of the place. It was a

22

cabin-lover's dream: notched logs, wide oak floors, bright throw rugs, and books to the ceiling on either side of the fireplace. I wandered over to examine them and sensed the familiar stirring of excitement aroused by the nearness of rows and rows of books. I was turning the pages of a collection of American short stories when he returned, carrying my wet clothes in a plastic bag.

I had read and enjoyed the identical book in college and was thinking of buying a copy. I opened my mouth to say something to that effect when he tossed the squishy bundle at my feet. "If you're ready?" he asked.

I was more than ready, and neither of us spoke as he led the way to his car. I looked at his straight silhouette in the dusk. It was a pity about his ears.

Five

It didn't occur to me until the following morning that I had forgotten to ask my reluctant host where to return the borrowed clothing. The idea of going back to that lake cabin made me stiffen with embarrassment. Never, *never* did I want to face that infuriating man again.

During the drive to town that morning I felt my confidence returning, the confidence that had been steadily eroding since the beginning of my quest. Maybe it was because of the sturdy, hot breakfast I had eaten or the exercise of the day before, but I felt eager, alive. I could almost sense the blood coursing through my body.

Despite its name and its menacing landmark, Raven Rock was a picture-book town, the kind an artist might like to paint. I pulled into a parking place across from the courthouse and inhaled the keen, early morning air. Roses bloomed on the courthouse lawn, thick, gnarled bushes planted long ago and tended carefully through the years. It was a good sign. I had searched in so many towns, so many courthouses, post offices, newspaper morgues, and cemetery records—all in mountain towns in North Carolina, and all near lakes. It was surprising how many there were. I had arrived in these towns with hope, left in despair. No one had ever heard of Maggie Grey; no one had known her. She was a phantom. Maybe she never existed. But if she didn't exist, then neither did I. It had been a negative, discouraging experience, until I came to Raven Rock and knew, through some mysterious magic, that Maggie Grey had lived there.

If my mother had voted in this county, the Board of Voter Registration would have proof of her having lived there. I had wasted precious hours in other towns visiting tax commissioners and other city officials to find that no records of this kind were kept over a certain period of time. Even if my mother had owned property, which was doubtful, evidence of this would be difficult to trace after so many years. Weeks of experience had honed my detective work to an exact art. Now I knew to go straight to the Board of Voter Registration. I had to depend on a hunch that Maggie Grey was a proper citizen and had registered to vote, and this time my hunch was right!

The busy clerk in the outer office provided me with the information as if it were the name of a reliable laundry. She found in five minutes the mother I had pursued from town to town during a long weary summer.

"Hold on just a minute now. I think I've found it!" She slammed the filing drawer with a twist of her ample hips. "Sure enough, here it is: Grey, Margaret R., registered twenty-four years ago in September." She studied me through heavy-rimmed glasses. "She a relative of yours?"

"Uh, no, just a friend of my mother's, a close friend. They lost touch, and Mother asked me if I'd look her up. They're planning a class reunion, and she was living here the last we heard." I smiled. My stomach felt as if I had swallowed lye, as if it were being eaten away. The clerk frowned. "Well, I doubt if this will do you much good. Twenty-four years is a long time, but I'll make a copy for you anyway. You never can tell, somebody still living out there might know where she went."

Outside the office I unfolded the square of slick, white paper with my mother's statistics machine-copied in pica type:

Grey   Margaret   R.

Sex: F   Hair: Brn.   Eyes: Brn.   Wt: 109

Ht. 5′ 3″   Race W

Is a registered Elector Of Glenn County
Resides at 344 English Street in the town of
Raven Rock, N. C. and is entitled to vote in
Raven Rock #1 Precinct

I wished that I had thought to ask the efficient clerk how to find English Street, but I hesitated to go back and inquire. I was sure she must have wondered why I would go to so much trouble for a class reunion. Could she tell that I was lying? Probably not, but I didn't want to push my luck.

A hurried man with a briefcase gave me sketchy directions when I cornered him in the hallway. I repeated them as I drove through the unfamiliar streets: "Right, four blocks. Left, two blocks. Then right again at supermarket," I muttered to myself. I sounded like a robot with mechanical difficulties. I found myself straining at the wheel, trying to push the car without going over the speed limit.

I passed a school, a massive brick building where workmen were painting trim, repairing an awning over the walk, getting ready for the school year just ahead. At the gray stone church on the corner, two ladies chatted leisurely as they strolled from the parking lot. Farther down the street, a plump, matronly woman attacked her dusty walk with wide, vigorous sweeps of the broom. It was an ordinary morning in an ordinary town. But not for me.

Then, there was the supermarket on the corner, and English Street just on the other side. I turned right slowly, palms sweating, eyes straining to read the street numbers on either side. I was in the eight-hundred block of a transitional section of town. What once had been residential was rapidly becoming commercial property. In between single-family dwellings were doctors' offices, small shops, and even a few apartment buildings. As the numbers crept lower, businesses thinned until English Street became a not-yet-shabby, still respectable neighborhood. The houses were old and set back from the road, protected from creeping commercialism by hedges or fences that needed paint.

Number 344 was next to a vacant lot at the corner of the wide, shady street. The roof peaked sharply behind the green-black foliage of a large magnolia. Clumps of fuchsia crepe myrtle trees splashed the dusky yard with brilliance. I slowed the car to an uneasy halt across the street from the house and unfolded a road map. With the pretense of being lost, I could study the building from a distance while I decided what to do.

Through the trees I could see a portion of the wide front porch and the angle of a gable at the top. It was a large, white frame house with just a hint of gingerbread trim. Had Maggie Grey lived here with her parents? Was this her family home? If so, were any of my relatives still living there?

It was large enough to be a rooming house, but I couldn't see a sign. Maybe rooming houses didn't advertise anymore. Which room had belonged to Maggie Grey, I wondered. Did she sit in the narrow dormer at night and watch for her lover through the branches of the dark magnolia? Was she happy there?

There was only one way to find out.

I stood in the street, wanting to cross, not wanting to cross. Did someone watch me from those shadowy windows? Was that someone Maggie Grey? I took one step, two. A wrought-iron lamp waited for darkness at the edge of the walk; iris bordered a stone birdbath in the shade of a twisted dogwood. The comfortable, snipping sound of the hedge clippers jolted me as someone began to trim the shrubbery on the far side of the house, someone who whistled. A man. My brother? My father?

I reached the opposite sidewalk. It was paved in flat, octagonal stones, broken through the years. If the child Maggie Grey had skated on them, they would have made a delightful, clacking noise, I thought. A waist-high stone wall with a paved cement top rose in square columns at the entrance. There was no gate, but there might as well have been one, a locked one. I could not go between those columns. I wanted to run up that shady walk, dash across the porch, pound on the door, but something held me back.

I stood, one hand still on the wall, one over my heart, as if I could calm the beating there. I wanted to go in that house. I had to go in that house. I had to find out if Maggie Grey had lived there. But someone, something was telling me to wait. It was almost as if I could hear a whisper in my ear. "Go back . . . go back . . . go back!" And I knew there was danger there.

Six

A defiant dandelion reared its shaggy head through a crack in the sidewalk at my feet. I stepped over it carefully, feeling a sisterhood with something so vulnerable.

The morning was almost gone, but not wasted. I had learned of my mother's previous address, also her height, weight, and coloring, which in itself was a victory over an unfulfilling summer. The house on English Street would have to wait. Why, I did not know; I only knew that it would.

If I were to stay in Raven Rock, which I knew I must, I would have to look for a job and a place to stay. And if the weekly newspaper wasn't impressed with my crisp, new journalism degree, I could always wait on tables, clerk in a store, anything that would give me an excuse to live in Raven Rock and bring in enough money to provide the essentials. I still had money from the sale of the furniture, as well as from Mom's share of the bakery, but I didn't want to use any more of it than I had to.

I had driven past the offices of the local newspaper the day before and was relieved to find that it hadn't run away or drifted off into space overnight, although I wouldn't have been surprised if it had!

The Raven Rock Register in bold, black letters on the dusty window had a distinctive look, a noble sound. Surely they would welcome someone with fresh ideas, someone like me.

I slid into a parking place, hardly able to believe my good luck in finding one directly in front of the office. As I wheeled happily into my slot, I realized that a man coming from the other direction was vying for the same position. The man in the battered, green Jeep stopped short, as if he could hardly believe what I had done. Grinning, I gave him a triumphant wave of my hand, which he ignored, scowling.

The scowl seemed familiar. The Jeep seemed familiar. Switching off my engine, I glanced over my shoulder as the car screeched away. Morgan Lawrence! Of all the people in Raven Rock, he was the last one I wanted to see! I shrugged. "You win some, you lose some," I said to the roar of his exhaust. The man was obviously a poor sport.

The Raven Rock Register had been in business for some time without changing its office decor. A dusty shade flapped as I opened the door on a crowded, paper-filled room that was divided into even smaller partitions by hip-high oak railings. The woman at the desk nearest the door was on the telephone. Skinny, with frizzled red hair and a large nose, she blinked at me, then raised a red-nailed finger in the direction of a chair. The chair had one bent leg, a year's layer of grime, and straw sticking out of the seat. I chose to stand. The receptionist continued her gum-smacking conversation in a monotone while sketching dainty hearts and flowers on a pad.

31

"Well, I don't know," she droned. "I just don't know if we can spare anybody just now. Well, I can check when he comes in. Ummm, yeah, all right, honey. We'll let you know tomorrow. That's okay. Bye now." The woman ripped the page from her pad and threw it in the trash can. "Can I help you?" She stared at me through blue-rimmed glasses, the kind that slant up at the ends.

I stepped forward, holding my portfolio like a shield. "Yes, I'm Henrietta Meredith, and I'd like to inquire about a job with your paper. I have newspaper experience and my degree in journalism."

She looked as if she didn't believe me.

"I have my résumé and some samples of my work here, if you'd like to see them." I offered the portfolio.

"No, that's okay." She began to rummage through drawers, sending papers flying.

I transferred my burden to one arm and leaned on the railing. It creaked. "Is the publisher in? If I could just talk with him . . . ?"

"Oh, he's hardly ever in! Mr. Smith lives in Atlanta." She looked at me as if I were not too bright and presented me with a dog-eared form. "The editor's the one you want to see, but he's not in either right now. Just fill this out, and I'll see that he gets it when he comes in."

"And when do you think that might be?" I asked.

She shrugged. "He's in and out, probably before noon, though."

I plopped an old newspaper in the chair and sat on it to fill out my form. She watched as I scribbled. I wished it were possible to list more under "Experience." This was my first job application in my field, and I wanted it to be perfect.

32

The red-haired receptionist scrutinized it carefully before taking it to an inner sanctum in the back. She was gone for a long time.

"The editor will see you now," she announced finally, opening the door a crack.

I had second thoughts as I gathered up my résumé; my apprehension was not unlike that which grows on one in the dentist's waiting room. I was aware that a journalism degree was no proof of writing ability, yet I knew I could write. But would the editor agree? I took a deep breath. The worst he could do was turn me down.

"Miss Cat Glasses" stepped aside to make room for me in the cubicle. Obviously she intended to linger. I wondered if the editor had come in a back way or if she had been lying. I suspected the latter.

"Thank you, Mildred." The man at the desk nodded his head toward the door, and Mildred scurried out. When I saw who he was, I wanted to scurry, too.

Morgan Lawrence leaned back in his chair. "Sit down, Miss Meredith."

I sat. "About that parking place . . . I guess it was yours?"

He nodded, holding my application form at arm's length, as though it might contaminate him. "I don't suppose you noticed the 'Reserved' sign on the curb?"

I felt like a kid in the principal's office. "I always seem to be saying, 'I'm sorry.' " I attempted a smile.

He sighed, rolling his eyes toward the ceiling. "It's all right, we have parking space in the back. Now," he sat up straighter, "let's get down to business. You need a job, right?"

I nodded. "Right."

Morgan Lawrence rapped a pencil on the desk. "I could use some help. The young man who was working for me moved on to greener pastures last month. So it happens you came at a good time, if you aren't too particular about what you do."

I frowned, wondering if the Peacock Café next door could use an inexperienced waitress. "I can write," I said.

He rattled my application. "I see you have a degree in journalism." He said it like: "I see you have poison ivy."

I untied my portfolio. "Here are some samples of my work: the college newspaper and the suburban weekly where I interned last year. I have some experience, but I'd like to have more." I sat straighter, trying to look as confident as possible under the circumstances.

Morgan Lawrence ruffled the samples of my journalistic endeavors and tossed them to one side. "Well, maybe we can unlearn some of this journalism school doctrine. At least, we can try." He looked at me through narrowed eyes. "Think you can write social news?"

"*Social news?*" My voice quaked. Be calm, Henrietta, I told myself. Don't blow this one. I cleared my throat. "I've never written social news, but I can try. Features are my specialty," I continued. "If you'd like to look at some of my clippings . . ."

I reached for the papers he had thrown so carelessly aside, my papers. His large, tan hand scooped them up, offered them to me. I grabbed at them, apparently too soon, because several of them ripped down the middle. I stood holding my half. "Well," I said, "so much for that."

His fingers brushed mine as he pried them gently from me. "Sit down, Miss Meredith. Please?"

"I didn't know anyone still called it 'social news,'" I began. "By that I guess you mean weddings, club meetings, things like that?" I'm sure the disgust showed on my face.

The editor laughed. "I know. It's awful, isn't it? But small-town subscribers expect it. In fact, if we omitted the society section, we'd lose half our readers." He sat on the edge of his desk. "Look, somebody has to do it. I don't have time. Mildred doesn't have . . . well, Mildred gets carried away. It wouldn't take much of your time, and you'd also be writing straight news." He smiled. "Listen, I know you want to conquer the world, but is there any reason you can't start right here at *The Register*?"

I looked at my shredded papers in his hand. "It seems as if I'll have to. That was my last copy of the college newspaper!"

"Good!" He crumpled it into a ball and shot it over his desk into the wastebasket. "I was counting on that. Can you start tomorrow?"

Seven

Tomorrow seemed a long way off as I backed out of my exclusive parking place later that day. (Sure enough, there was a "Reserved" sign on the curb in faded red letters!) I had been introduced to the rest of the office staff, which was composed of five people: an advertising manager, Linotype operator, printer, Mildred, and a Mrs. Saxon, who came in several days a week to read proof. Charlie Rogers, the droll, grizzled advertising manager, I liked at once, and the others seemed a likeable assortment. In time, I supposed, I would even get used to Mildred. As for Morgan Lawrence, I intended to stay as far away from him as possible.

I spent the rest of the day looking for a place to live. The classified section of *The Register* offered a limited selection of rental property. I found that I had a choice of a seedy-looking trailer, a terrace apartment (which turned out to be a leaky basement), or pitching a tent. Of the three, I favored the tent. The expense of taking all my meals out, plus the modest motel fee, was eating into my savings, and the sterile, boxlike room I lived in was a far cry from home.

I entered my little partition the next morning with clenched teeth in preparation for the boring task of writing society news. Our section of the office area was one step lower than the rest—I wondered if there were a significance to this—and the surrounding railings gave it the appearance of a playpen. I had a desk, typewriter, chair, wastebasket, and filing cabinet. The dark floors, oiled with time and grime, creaked with every other step. I planted my pocketbook in the dust on top of the filing cabinet and eased into my chair. There was just enough room between the desk and the wall if I didn't gain any weight. I had been instructed to type up club notices from information that had been collected, a test of my skills, I suspected. The typewriter was a sturdy manual with a muscle-building carriage. It was a bulky, bossy, no-nonsense machine with a bell loud enough to wake the dead. I had found my first friend.

I typed for about an hour, absorbing the pungent smell of printer's ink, the musty, dusty, vital smell of that essential American organ, the newspaper. The clicks and clacks, bells and voices in the background blended into a heartbeat in rhythm with my own, and for the first time in months I felt at home.

"You're working too hard on your first day! Come on and have a cup of coffee before you show us up." Patricia Saxon leaned on the railings of my cubicle. "Better than that, I'll bring you some. Cream and sugar?"

I was ready for a break and glad of an opportunity to talk with someone, especially another woman. I accepted the coffee gratefully. "Thanks! I'd offer you a chair, but . . ."

"That's okay. I'll just sit here on the edge of your cage." Pat had an ageless, even-featured face, but I imagined her to be in her thirties. She had taken the part-time proofreading job in order to earn a little extra money now that her children were all in school. She smiled over her cup. "Cheers!"

I tasted the coffee. It was perfect. "This is great," I said. "I can really appreciate good coffee after eating at the motel. The food's not bad, but their coffee . . . Ugh!"

Pat stood to stretch her lanky legs. "I know, I've tried it. Morgan makes this. Puts it on first thing every morning. It tastes a lot better than mine."

I had enjoyed Morgan Lawrence's coffee on another occasion. It was his best, and probably his only, asset.

Pat rested an elbow against the filing cabinet. "Are you planning on staying there long?"

"The motel? Not if I can help it!" I ran a finger through the dust on my desk. "But it doesn't look like I'm going to find an apartment. I've looked everywhere. There's nothing to rent."

"Hey, what about that duplex on Dorsey Street? It looks okay, close in, too."

I shook my head. "Too late. I called yesterday. It's rented."

"They don't last long around here." Pat folded her arms. "Let me think a minute. Have you tried Essie's?"

"Essie's? What's that?"

"A rooming house, and not far from here, either. All the teachers used to live there."

"Whoopee! Sounds exciting." I savored the last taste of my coffee.

Pat raised an eyebrow. "Food's good, and it's cheap."

I reached for the phone. "What's her number?"

She placed a restraining hand on my arm. "Wait a minute. That's not the way."

I frowned. "What do you mean?"

"Essie's particular," Pat explained. "She doesn't take just anybody. She has to know you, like you."

I shrugged. "Guess that lets me out."

"Not necessarily. She likes me. My mother used to sew for her, made most of her clothes. And I know most of the boarders out there too, went to school while they were still teaching."

"It would help," I said, "if you went with me, as sort of a reference. Would you mind?"

Pat pulled at a strand of short, dark hair, twisting the straight wisps around her finger. "Glad to, but I know somebody who would be even better."

"Who?"

"Morgan! Essie thinks he's God or something. He runs her little features now and then. You know, cooking and recipes and stuff. You'll probably have to edit them. She can't type, and her handwriting's terrible."

"I don't know," I said. "I doubt if he . . ."

"Doubt if who what?" Morgan Lawrence stood in the entrance to my office.

"Henri's having trouble finding a place to live," Pat explained. "I was telling her that, with your recommendation, she might to able to get a room at Essie's."

If I read them correctly, Morgan's eyes were flashing, "fat chance" in green neon. "Why Essie's?" he asked.

"Does she have any choice?" Pat's eyes narrowed. "How would you like living at the Raven Rock Motel?"

I let out a deep breath. I had found an ally in Pat Saxon.

Morgan Lawrence turned to me as if he hadn't heard her and held out a giant hand. "Could I have those club notes now, Miss Meredith?"

I passed them on silently, as Pat stared openmouthed. "Is he always this rude?" I asked, as his office door clicked shut.

Pat shrugged, "Well, he's kind of short sometimes. Abrupt, if you know what I mean, but never as rude as that!" She stared at me in disbelief. "It's you, Henri! What have you done to him?"

I told her, recounting the events on my fingers, of my dip in the stream, my soggy invasion of his precious solitude, complete with details of the silent ride home with my bike wedged in the back of the Jeep.

She blinked. "You're making that up!"

"And yesterday," I added, "I snatched his parking place, right from under his nose."

Pat clamped a hand to her eyes. "Oh, no! He's very possessive about that space!"

I nodded. "So I noticed."

She didn't answer. She was shaking silently. "I'm sorry," she mumbled, doubling over in a new fit of laughter. "Oh, I wish I had seen that! If only I had been looking out the window."

"Humph!" I snorted. "You'd have to wash it first."

"Miss Meredith!" His voice bellowed from the sacred chamber. "Could you come in here for a minute, please?"

Pat dabbed at her eyes. "You've only been here an hour, and the place has livened up already. If I don't see you again, it certainly has been an interesting experience." She was still quivering.

The editor leaned back in his chair, his eyes fixed on a point on the ceiling. His desk looked as if someone had emptied a trash can over it.

"The club news will do fine," he announced, swinging around to face me. "You can take this on back to the composing room."

I studied the copy. "But what about headlines? Do you want me to write them, or will you take care of it?"

"Bud will add them when he sets up the page."

"Bud?"

"The printer. He was in this business long before we were. Unless it's something special, I leave the makeup to him, except for ads, of course."

I nodded dumbly. They didn't tell us about situations like this in journalism school.

Morgan Lawrence grinned. "Does that surprise you?"

"A little," I admitted.

"Well, I have another surprise. How would you like to be a teacher?"

"Are you trying to tell me I'm fired?"

"Hell no, woman!" He didn't look as fierce when he laughed. "I thought you could use the added income, if you don't mind a little extra work. And it would get Joyce McDonald off my back."

I blinked. "Teach what? Who's Joyce McDonald?" I would have considered sitting if I could have found a chair, but it was buried in the debris.

"You sound like a parrot. Joyce is an old friend of mine, a teacher at the middle school." He jerked a briefcase, a dictionary, and an ink-smeared towel from the seat of the extra chair and offered me the space. "They're starting a program for gifted children this year, and it will include a class in journalism, that is, if you're interested."

I smiled. "I'm interested."

"You'll be helping them to get out a school paper," he went on. "The class only meets twice a week. You should be able to work it into your lunch hour.

"Oh, you'll have some extra time to eat," he added, seeing my face, "and about a hundred more a month from the school." He studied my reaction. "You like kids?"

My eagerness should have been obvious. "Yes, yes, I do. And I'd really like to help with this. It sounds like fun."

"Well, possibly." His eyes held a doubtful gleam. "But, remember, you'll have them by yourself, probably as many as twenty. They're bright kids, but they're kids, still fall in creeks and stuff like that, not a whole lot younger than you are."

I pretended not to see his grin. "I think I can manage."

"Good!" He grew serious. "The school needs this program. I hope you can make it work. We can't pay much here, and I thought the extra money might make up for it."

His words were sincere, and I felt myself not really liking the man, but disliking him less. "Don't tell the school board," I said, "but I probably would have done it for nothing."

"Oh, Miss Meredith," he added as I prepared to leave, "I hope you haven't made plans for lunch. I telephoned Essie, and she's expecting us at one. Better work up an appetite because she's a darn good cook!"

Eight

Before we turned down English Street, I had been hungry, ready for one of Essie's renowned meals, but now I was turning into a granite statue. Statues don't eat. It was an apprehensive feeling, as if some power I couldn't explain was hurtling me toward an unknown destination—somewhere I didn't want to go. We drove through the gray-green tunnel of trees that lined the drive at 344 English Street, just as I knew we would. Morgan Lawrence parked the Jeep at the side of the house and leaped over the side, waiting for me to join him. There were flagstones leading to a porch in the front. I knew that the fourth one from the steps would be broken in three places, and it was. And there was something else familiar, a gnawing reminder, like a buzzing in my ears. From this angle of the house I recognized the porch with the diamond-shaped pattern on the banisters. It was the house in the photograph, my photograph!

My hand went instinctively to my heart. The photograph! When was the last time I had seen it? Then I remembered the bike ride to Raven Rock Lake, the plunge into the creek. The picture had been in the pocket of my shirt, and the shirt was stuffed in the bottom of a pillow case waiting to be laundered. The photograph had probably disintegrated by now.

I must have hesitated at the steps. Morgan Lawrence pressed my arm. "Nervous?" He glanced toward the door.

I tried to smile. "I feel as if I'm about to be auditioned."

"Don't worry. We're just home folks here." He pushed open the door without knocking, letting the screen slam behind us.

"Morgan! Nice to see you!" A stocky, balding man greeted us. He offered his hand, smiling. "I'm Howard Lucas." Aside he whispered, "It's good to have a pretty face around here for a change. Hope you'll be joining us often."

"Howard clerks at Wayne's Hardware," Morgan explained. "Women don't come in there often, you know. He gets carried away when he sees one, so you'd better watch out!"

I laughed as Howard shrugged. "He knows me too well," he said.

We stood in a wide hallway that appeared even wider because of its white wainscoting and magnolia-print wallpaper. A massive oak staircase rose behind us. The treads squeaked as two elderly ladies descended, their small feet lightly touching the moss-green carpet.

My first impression of the Waverly sisters was of a reversible rag doll that is smiling on one side and frowning on the other. Well into their seventies, the two had been retired from teaching for several years and now spent most of their time arguing, Morgan later explained.

"Why, Morgan Lawrence!" Miss Carrie's blue-gray head reached just above his elbow. "How did you know we were having sweet potato custard today?" Her baby-blue eyes were wide and sweet, her face almost unlined.

"Carrie, that was yesterday we had the sweet potato custard!" Her sister, of identical size and coloring, jostled her elbow. Miss Cora's sapphire eyes were shrewd, her mouth pinched. "She can't even remember what she ate one day ago!" she remarked in a loud voice.

"But I would remember if I ate sweet potato pie, Sister," Miss Carrie said sweetly.

I turned at the sound of footsteps behind me. "Are you two at it again? For goodness' sakes, leave poor Morgan alone and give him a chance to introduce his guest." A tall, smiling woman wiped her hands on her apron and enclosed my cold hands in her large, warm ones. "Welcome to Raven Rock. I'm Essie Honeycutt."

I think I would have known her anywhere. She was as familiar to me as a well-learned poem, a comfortable melody. A large, flushed matriarch of the boarding-house, she bustled with spontaneity. Essie gave my hand a damp squeeze. "I know you must be hungry. We're running a little late today." She patted my arm briefly as we moved into the dining room, and I noticed that her hands were freckled from dishwater, as Mom's had been. It was a little thing, but enough to bring tears to my eyes.

I watched them as they filed into the room, searched each boarder for a look of Maggie Grey. But my mother wasn't there. I had sensed it from the moment I walked through the door. Perhaps she had once lived in this house, eaten at this table. But Maggie Grey was gone. Gone where? I had to know.

Essie's tall son Seth brought in the heavy platter of roast beef and took his place at the end of the table. Judging from the few strands of gray in his dark-brown hair, I gathered that he must be in his late thirties or early forties. Seth Honeycutt was a nice-looking man, reflecting his mother's easy grace and charm. I caught his dark eyes probing mine as he teased me about my job.

"You've come to the right town if you're expecting to uncover sensational scandal," he said as he served my plate. "Why, just last month they caught the preacher's daughter smoking pot behind the gym!"

Howard Lucas laughed. "And don't forget the burglary!"

Morgan put down his fork. "What burglary?"

Howard broke open a steaming biscuit. "Why, haven't you heard? Somebody sneaked into Dunagan's store the other day and lifted every piece of bubble gum in the jar!"

Morgan shook his head. "It's not always that dull, Henrietta, I promise."

Essie looked up from her greens. "He's right, I guess. There's meanness here, same as anywhere, maybe even more."

"I think people are getting meaner everywhere," Miss Cora said. "The whole world's going crazy!"

"Oh, Sister, now!" I noticed that Miss Carrie sat at the other end of the table, as far away from her sister as she could get. I didn't blame her.

Besides the two sisters and Howard Lucas, the only permanent roomer present was Amos Tomlinson, a stooped, sorrowful-looking widower who had recently sold his home. I could understand how he felt and tried to make conversation with him, but he made it clear that he didn't want to talk. Roberta Gardner, the plump, cow-faced bank teller who sat at my right, confessed that she looked forward to feasting at Essie's every working day.

The food was delicious. I could understand why Roberta enjoyed her lunch hour. After observing what Essie's food had done to Roberta's figure, I should have declined dessert, but I took one look at the banana pudding and turned into a spineless jellyfish. I wasn't sorry.

"And what made you decide on Raven Rock, Henrietta?" Essie refilled my coffee cup for the third time.

I stirred the cream in slowly. "I heard there was a vacancy here, so I grabbed it." I wasn't telling a lie. The editor of the paper in the next county had mentioned the opening when I had inquired there.

She smiled. "It's just that we're such a little, out-of-the-way place. I hope you won't be lonely here."

"Oh, no!" I was quick to assure her. "In fact, it's just what I was looking for." I turned to Morgan. "Mr. Lawrence will tell you, newspaper jobs are hard to find right now. I'm lucky to have one."

"Just remember that," he reminded me, "when you have to write society!"

I took a sip of coffee to fortify my courage. "Pat Saxon suggested that I might find a room here with you. I've been staying at the motel, so you can see why I'm eager to find something more permanent."

Essie Honeycutt refolded her napkin. "Oh, I see. I wish we could offer you a place, Henrietta, but there just isn't a room left. We haven't had a vacancy since Mr. Tomlinson moved in with us last year."

Seth reached for his cigarettes. "I can understand your situation. I'm on the road a lot. I have to travel in my work as a salesman, and it's tough finding a place to stay in these little towns."

Miss Carrie dabbed daintily at her pink mouth. "Have you tried the Lake Forest, dear?"

47

Her sister groaned. "Carrie, they tore that old hotel down two years ago!"

"Did they? What a pity! They served such good shortcake. Remember that shortcake, Essie?" Miss Carrie blinked.

"There's always Mrs. Blakenship's." Roberta Gardner scooped the last piece of banana from her dish. "Doesn't she rent rooms sometimes?"

"Amanda Blakenship?" Miss Cora sat up with a jerk. "Why, she'd freeze to death over there! She keeps the thermostat on fifty."

"It wouldn't do, Henrietta," Morgan agreed. "You wouldn't like it."

The motel was beginning to sound like a palace to me.

Seth leaned back in his chair and blew a lazy swirl of smoke. "There is one place." He watched his mother's face. "Why couldn't she stay in Honeysuckle House?"

Essie Honeycutt's napkin fell unheeded to the floor. "But, Seth, that's been empty for years! No, I don't want . . . I don't think . . ." She looked from Morgan to me. "We use it for storage. It's full of junk, and there's no telling what kind of shape it's in."

Seth frowned. "There's nothing wrong with Honeysuckle House, Mother. Nothing at all."

Essie shook her head. "No, it wouldn't be suitable at all. I don't know why you even suggested it."

"It's all right." I tried to keep my voice from shaking. "I'm sure I can find another place." If she had slapped my face, I couldn't have been more hurt. Essie Honeycutt didn't want me there.

Nine

I was ready to start back to *The Register* as soon as we left the table, but Morgan was holding court on a chintz-covered throne in the living room, chatting with Howard Lucas as if he were a long-lost brother. The Waverly sisters and Roberta Gardner hovered near, to lap up their share of attention.

I browsed. The watercolor prints were contributed by an art teacher back in the sixties, Essie pointed out, the hand-painted bookcase constructed by another past resident. And the high school annual on the end table was dedicated to the long-suffering Miss Emma Pike (rest her soul), who taught history for thirty-five years. I flipped through the pages, half smiling at the crew cuts and Peter Pan collars, penny loafers and letter-sweaters. There was enough hair spray used by the senior class alone to hold up a building.

Her face smiled up at me from the faculty section: large, laughing, brown eyes; soft, dark hair; straight nose, but short, like mine. Margaret R. Grey, Home Economics.

I don't know how long I stood there staring at the page; my gaze locked into the picture, absorbing every detail of her face. It was a young face. It seemed younger even than some of her students. I looked back at the date on the front: the year before I was born. Had she known then of her pregnancy? There was no clue in the serenity of her smile.

A shadow fell across the page, and I turned to find Seth Honeycutt standing behind me.

"If you can tear yourself away from Miss Emma's annual, I'll give you the grand tour," he offered.

I wanted to clasp the book to me and run, to tell him to go away. It was not a moment to share. But he was smiling, polite, trying to make a stranger feel at home. I had no choice. I let the book snap shut, quickly replaced it on the table, and pretended to welcome the opportunity to get outside.

We walked through the sunny, cluttered kitchen and paused on the latticed back porch. I wondered how many bushels of peas had been shelled there, how many ears of corn shucked. It was that kind of place. Did my mother ever sit here on a warm autumn afternoon, laughing over the incidents of the day, dropping peas into a pan? There was room for restful chatter on the porch, as in the rest of the rambling house. The Honeycutt house, like many others built in the early 1900s, had been designed without concern for wasted space. It was the kind of house that should have had a fern stand on the landing, a window seat under the dormers, bathtubs on legs.

No grass grew under the huge water oak at the back door. There should have been a swing there. Seth glanced at me quizzically as we stepped outside. "You like it, don't you?"

I looked back at the venerable building where ruffled curtains hung behind rippling glass panes. "It has a gracious character," I began. And yet there was something else, an elusive quality that shut me out, excluded me.

His eyes narrowed. "It soaks up paint like a sponge, and the heat goes right to the ceiling. Still," he shrugged, "it's home. My grandmother was born here." He took my arm. "Like scuppernongs? Come and see the arbor."

Heavy vines clung to the sagging, wooden trellis, creating a dark, green cave for decaying wooden seats. I sucked the pulp from a thick-skinned green grape, relishing its tart, plumlike flavor.

"They make excellent wine." Seth rolled the fruit into my palm, reserving one for himself. "Mother puts up a few quarts every year. We keep it in a secret place." He winked. "Miss Carrie is a little too fond of it."

I laughed. "I don't believe you! Not that sweet, little old lady."

At one side of the arbor was the garage, which, Seth pointed out, was just large enough for a Model T. A narrow path ran behind this to a yellow stone building almost hidden by trees. "Honeysuckle House," Seth explained. "We've always called it that because of the color of the stones and the vines around it. It has its entrance on the other street."

The house had a shuttered, abandoned look. Trapped in a tangle of vines, barricaded by trees, it stood in shadows where sunlight never strayed. A chill went through me. I made some nonsensical comment and turned to go.

Seth touched my arm. "Well, what do you say? Think you'd like living here?"

I rubbed my bare arms to keep warm. "I think your mother settled that at dinner. Honeysuckle House is not for rent."

He smiled, resting his hand on my shoulder. "Henrietta, I hope you weren't hurt by what my mother said. Believe me, it wasn't because of anything you did or said. She'll come around."

"She sounded definite to me." I examined the cottage over his shoulder. "And she's probably right. Look at it! It isn't fit to be lived in. How long has it been since anyone stayed there?"

He shoved his hands in his pockets. "A while, but it's a good house. It was built for a guest house, I think. I was born here. This is where my parents started housekeeping. Then later, when my grandmother grew older, we moved in the main house to be with her. I must have been about six then."

I stared at the vine-wrapped chimney. "You mean it's been empty since *then?*"

He laughed. "Oh, no! It was rented for a while, but it didn't work out."

"What do you mean?"

He frowned. "There was some unpleasantness. One of the girls was killed."

"Killed! Here, at the cottage?" I shuddered.

"Oh no! A tramp attacked her on the street." He shrugged. "It all happened years ago. I don't remember the details, but Mother does. It left her with bitter memories about Honeysuckle House. That's why she won't talk about it, won't set foot inside." He touched my hand. "Please don't let her know I told you this. I don't like to remind her, and maybe it's cruel of me, but it's time she learned to deal with this phobia." He waved an arm. "It's a good, solid house. It could be painted, repaired, lived in. I hate to see it standing here like this, wasting away! We don't need it, but you do." His hands gripped my shoulders. "What do you say, Henrietta, will you think about it?"

52

A blaring horn jarred the silence, jolted me from the spell of the honey-stoned house. "I really have to go, Seth." I took a few halting steps back the way we had come, leaving him there in the shadows staring wistfully at the little house. He made no move to follow. "Seth!" My voice broke into his reverie. "I'm leaving now," I said.

He lifted a hand in salute. "I'll call you about the cottage."

I hurried toward the Jeep, where Morgan Lawrence impatiently raced the motor, and called a hasty good-bye to the few diners who remained in the living room, and to Essie, thanking her for my meal. She kissed my cheek as we parted, whispering softly in my ear. I was in a hurry, and Morgan was making so much noise with the car, I wondered if I had heard her correctly. It had sounded as if Essie had warned me. "Be careful," she said. I puzzled over her words as we drove back to town, finally deciding I was letting my imagination run away with me again.

Ten

I found the damp shirt in a wad at the bottom of the pillowcase under three days of dirty laundry; it was mud-streaked and sour. I scrambled for the pocket, dreading what I would find.

The pocket was empty. I could see that, but I searched anyway, jamming my fingers inside—nothing!

I sank into the only chair in my motel room and tried to think. The pocket flap had been unbuttoned. Had I taken the picture out when I changed clothes at the cabin? I couldn't remember. If I had left it in the bedroom, Morgan Lawrence would surely have found it. I had to know, then, that night. I couldn't wait another day.

I riffled the pages of the phone book, noting that two Lawrences were listed at the same address, not the cabin at the lake, but a residence in town: Morgan and a Dr. John Lawrence. My fingers slipped, tangled in the dial, but finally it rang. I looked at my watch. It was almost six. They were probably at dinner.

A woman's voice answered. (The one whose jeans I had borrowed?) I heard the clatter of silverware, the sound of a chair being pushed back, and Morgan answered curtly. I apologized for interrupting his meal and came right to the point.

"Picture?" He sounded as if he were still chewing and not bothering to disguise it. "You mean that old snapshot made in front of Essie's? I didn't know that was yours."

I explained that the photograph had belonged to my mother, that one of the members of the group had been a friend of hers, and she had asked me to look her up. I don't think I sounded convincing. There was a silence on the other end of the line, a long silence. "Funny that she should know someone who lived here," he said finally. "I thought it was an old picture of Dad's. Strange, I didn't realize you knew anyone here." His words had a doubting quality.

I repeated that I *hadn't* known the woman, had never seen her, but I hated to lose the photograph. "Would you remember any of those people?" I tried to maintain a casual tone.

"Probably. I really didn't look at it, to tell you the truth. I thought Dad had been in one of his nostalgic moods and had forgotten to put it away. Look, I'll bring it to you tomorrow. I think I know where it is." He was eager to get back to his dinner. "You won't need it before then?"

"Oh, no! Tomorrow will be fine." I laughed to convey the insignificance of the matter. "Just thought I'd better call while it was on my mind, before I forgot."

As if I could forget, I thought, hanging up the receiver. I regretted the incident about the picture, regretted the necessity of calling. I would have preferred that no one in Raven Rock knew of my connection there. The story about my mother's friend was the one I had concocted for the clerk at the Board of

55

Voter Registration, and I doubted if Morgan Lawrence accepted it. I was not a good liar.

Morgan was not at *The Register* office when I arrived the next morning. (I soon learned that he spent more time away from his desk than behind it.) I tried to control my impatience, forced myself to remain seated every time someone opened the door. The endless details of a wedding were on my desk with a memo from Morgan reminding me that jobs in my profession were hard to find. I jerked the cover from my mammoth typewriter and rolled in the copy paper.

When our editor did arrive, I was so bogged down in adjectives, I didn't even know he was there until my gate creaked open.

"What's another word for 'charming'?" I glanced up to meet his grin. "I've already used: 'lovely,' 'elegant,' 'graceful,' and 'exquisite,' and I'm beginning to feel nauseated."

He frowned at the copy in my typewriter. "Don't you think you should save some for the next wedding?"

I groaned. "I wish every girl in Raven Rock would stay an old maid! I can't go through this again."

"I'll tell you what." He started to leave. "I'll loan you my thesaurus."

"Oh, wait! Did you remember to bring the snapshot?"

He frowned, rumpling his hair. "The . . . oh, you know, that's the strangest thing! I could have sworn I put that picture in the glove compartment of my Jeep, but . . ."

"You didn't find it?" I hoped he couldn't read my expression.

"Oh, it's around somewhere, has to be. It's probably still at the cabin. I'm sure it will turn up." He frowned. "Look, Henrietta, I'm sorry. I hope it wasn't too important."

I shrugged. "No, it's okay. I just hate to lose it. It was the only one Mom had, of this friend of hers, I mean."

He nodded. "I see. Well, I'll look again. We'll find it sooner or later.

"Oh, by the way," Morgan paused. "Joyce called. If you can spare an hour or so this morning, they'd like you to come by the school to discuss this program."

I rolled in another sheet of paper. "It shouldn't take long to write up these bridal parties. Is there anything else that needs to be done before I go?"

"Nothing urgent. Just be back before two."

"What happens at two?"

He rubbed his hands together, making a steeple of his fingers. "VIP in town. Want you to get an interview."

I felt a shiver of excitement. The governor? A bestselling author? Maybe a noted performer? "Don't keep me in suspense," I said.

He looked at the floor, his mouth twitching. "Mrs. Edwin T. Prescott."

"Mrs. *who?*"

"Mrs. Edwin T. Prescott." He puffed out his chest. "State president of the American Federation of Women's Clubs. She'll be speaking at the civic center at two. Think you can handle it?"

I would have thrown my typewriter at him, but I couldn't lift it.

Raven Rock Middle School was not the enormous brick structure I had passed on my way to English Street, but a smaller building very much like it a few blocks away. The corridor smells of floor polish and fresh paint were overpowered by the ever-prevailing schoolhouse aroma of chalk dust, wet raincoats, and forgotten bananas. It made me feel three feet tall.

The school secretary announced my arrival to Joyce McDonald over a complicated communications system that resembled the control panel of a jet plane. It not only looked like one, but buzzed, shrieked, and crackled accordingly. The secretary laughed at my startled expression. "Warming up for the school year," she explained. "I'm Fran Oliver." She extended a slender hand. "You must be Henrietta Meredith. Welcome to middle school."

"I admire your technological skills," I said, accepting her offer of a chair. I glanced behind me at the empty hallway. "It's so quiet around here!"

Fran Oliver lifted an eyebrow. "Just you wait until next week! Enjoy it while it lasts." She filled two paper cups from an ancient urn and offered me coffee.

"Good! I see you've been served. Fran, is there any more of that mess?" Joyce McDonald was a square, solidly built woman in her late forties with a mop of short, graying curls. She flinched at the taste of the bitter coffee and nodded toward an inner door. "Is *she* in?"

Fran tapped her cup with a finger. "Who did you think made the coffee?"

Joyce introduced herself to me by dumping a sheaf of papers in my lap. "Your students," she explained, "names, ages, grades, interests, and other immaterial information. Our job will be to get them interested in creating something of their own before they atrophy from an overdose of television. I'm Joyce McDonald."

I steadied the papers with one hand and balanced my cup in the other. "I'd shake your hand," I began, "but . . ."

Her smile accented the laugh lines at the corners of her eyes. Her skin looked weathered, as if she spent a lot of time outdoors. "Bring your cup with you. I want you to meet the boss!"

The boss was Bertie Hammondtree, an armor-plated autocrat whose sixty (or more) years were obvious, in spite of the facade of glowing hair (Tawny Gold #2, guaranteed not to shampoo out). Her sharp, blue eyes impaled me, and I stared at the wall. I had a ridiculous feeling that she would be able to read my thoughts if I met her gaze. I didn't think there would be many discipline problems at Raven Rock Middle School.

There would be a fifty-minute journalism class each Tuesday and Thursday, I was informed. My eighteen students had been selected according to talent and performance from all three grades of the school (five to seven), and we were to "publish" a mimeographed paper at the end of every month. Mrs. McDonald would be available to assist and advise me whenever necessary. The principal indicated my patron with a queenly nod. Did I have any questions? (If I had any, I wouldn't have dared to ask them!) We were dismissed.

Fran looked up from her typing and lifted her cold coffee in salute. "You have just been baptized by steel and fire."

My knees were shaking. "I don't feel so well," I said. "I must be coming down with something, probably something fatal."

Joyce laughed. "You can't escape that easily! We have at least two members on this faculty who have been dead for years, and they're still teaching." She clamped a hearty hand on my shoulder. "You'll get used to her. She's not so bad. I doubt if you'll see much of her."

I sat down. "Oh, Lord, I hope not!"

Joyce glanced at her watch. "Come on, I'll show you around the school, and we'll go to my place for a sandwich. The cafeteria's not open yet."

The phone rang as we were leaving the office. Fran waved us back. "It's for you," she said.

"Henrietta?" I didn't recognize his voice at first. "Seth Honeycutt. Morgan said I might find you there. I've finally convinced Mother to see the light! What color do you want your house?"

Eleven

"So, you're going to live in Honeysuckle House!" Joyce said again as she slapped mayonnaise on thick slabs of bread.

I munched on a potato chip. "I *might* live in Honeysuckle House."

She dumped some pickles in a dish. "I know I must sound like a broken record, but that little place holds a lot of memories for me. I didn't know they rented it anymore."

"They didn't. Seth talked his mother into letting me use it. In a way, I wish he hadn't."

Joyce licked a finger. "Why not?"

I shrugged. "It has kind of a sad history from what Seth says."

"Yes, I guess it does. I'm surprised Seth remembers that. He must have been away at school then." She reached for more bread. "I don't think of it that way, though. Dan and I had most of our dates there. We couldn't afford to go anywhere else."

"You dated at Honeysuckle House?" I must have looked puzzled.

Joyce dealt paper plates like a poker hand. "Sure, I lived there."

I frowned. "But I thought no one lived in the cottage after . . ." Realization hit me. "You roomed with the girl who was killed?"

Joyce looked at me over her glass of tea. "Did he tell you about that? Yes, I shared it with two other girls. I only lived there for a few months, until Dan and I married. It's a nice little place, with a fireplace." She laughed. "Dan will tell you about the time we built a fire with the damper shut!" She looked up. "Here he is. I thought he'd probably come home for lunch."

Dan McDonald's lean frame towered over his wife as he bent to kiss her cheek. Joyce explained about my journalism class as she introduced me to her husband.

He smiled as we shook hands. "I hope we can have something like that next year at the junior high. Think you could work it out?"

"I don't know," I said. "It depends on what the principal's like. Miss Bertie's about all I can handle right now."

Joyce and her husband exchanged glances and began to laugh.

"Oh, no!" I almost choked on my tea. "Don't tell me you're . . ."

He nodded. "Right! And don't let Miss Bertie scare you. That's exactly what she wants."

"Well, she certainly succeeded," I said.

"Henri's going to live in Honeysuckle House," Joyce explained. "I was telling her what it was like when I lived there. Remember?"

Dan was slicing a tomato. The knife stopped halfway through. "Really? I didn't know Essie let that place anymore."

"It will have to have some repairs," I said. "The roof is slate, so that's okay, but of course it needs painting inside. Seth thinks it needs to be lived in."

"I agree." Joyce smiled. "We'll help, won't we, Dan? We'll have a painting party, just like before we were married." She turned to me. "You furnish the beer, Henri. We'll furnish the labor." She sighed. "Gosh, it's been a long time since I was in that house!"

Her husband grinned. "Now come on, we're not that old!"

"Maybe you can find a roommate, Henri," Joyce suggested. "It's more fun if you have someone to share it, and it does sit back away from the main house. You won't be afraid there alone, will you?"

I watched Dan wolf down his second sandwich and wondered where he put it all. "It would be nice if I could find someone compatible. You were lucky to have two agreeable friends. That must have been terrible for you when your roommate was killed. Does the other girl still live here?"

Dan's eyes met hers for a flicker of a second, and Joyce looked down at her plate. "No, no she doesn't. How about some more tea?"

I shook my head. "I'm sorry. It must bother you to talk about it."

"No. Not now, not like it did." She broke a potato chip in half and dropped the pieces in her plate. "You see, that happened after I married. The months I spent in Honeysuckle House were happy ones, for all of us. We were all teachers," she explained. "Essie's always been particular about her roomers. I guess she thinks teachers are more or less respectable!" She laughed. "Anyway, I was teaching in the elementary school, and Nell and Maggie in the high school." She paused, turning her tea glass in circles. "Nell was the one who was killed," she said finally. "It happened in the spring, some maniac. They finally convicted him." Her voice was shaking. "I didn't want to frighten you. It had nothing to do with Honeysuckle House."

I stared at the sandwich crust, the half-eaten pickle on my plate as if I had never seen them before. "And Maggie?" I asked. "What happened to her?"

"She left not long after that," Dan explained. "Soon after the beginning of the fall term, wasn't it, Joyce?"

His wife nodded. "It was the strangest thing. I never did feel right about it. Maggie Grey and I were as close as sisters. I thought I knew her better than anyone, yet she never said a word about going, never let me know where she went. She just left."

Didn't you know she was pregnant? I wanted to ask. Didn't you know she had a lover, my father? I looked at Dan, the right age, in his early fifties. Although his hair was graying, it was still reddish-brown like mine, russet, Mom had called it. Could it have been Dan? I focused my attention on the ice in my glass, swirled it around. "Perhaps something was worrying her," I said. "Romantic problems, maybe. Was she dating anyone?"

Joyce smiled. "Oh, Maggie had a lot of dates, a string of fellows, but no one in particular. Of course, after Dan and I married, I didn't see her as much as before, and we were away all that summer. There could have been someone. I don't know."

"And you never heard from her again?"

She shook her head. "No, and just after she left, her parents came here asking about her. They didn't know where she was either. I think she must have had an argument with her father. He was old to be her father, and very strict. They had different ideas about things." Joyce turned to Dan. "I wonder if Maggie's parents are still living? I've often thought about getting in touch, just to find out where she is. What's the name of that little town they lived in? Shannon, wasn't it? Seems like they lived on a farm."

I was aware of Dan's gaze as I helped Joyce clear the table. "Funny, but you remind me of Maggie some," he said finally.

"Who?" Joyce paused at the refrigerator.

"Henri. She's something like Maggie, don't you think?"

Joyce frowned. "Well, maybe a little. You must have reminded me of her, Henri. I haven't thought of Maggie in months. I hope we didn't bore you with our reminiscing. We must be getting old!"

"No, I wasn't bored." I forced my voice to sound calm.

"We didn't intend to bring up such a gloomy subject," Joyce continued, "but I guess you were bound to hear about it sooner or later. Nothing has ever happened like that before or since." She frowned. "Probably that's why Maggie left, because of what happened to Nell. I think she was afraid of the Chuckler."

"The *who*?" I asked.

"The Chuckler," she explained. "That's what the murderer called himself. His intended victims, the ones who got away, said he chuckled just before he attacked. He wore some sort of clown mask."

"But they arrested him," Dan said. "He was safely behind bars. Why should she still be afraid?"

Joyce faced her husband. "And why should Maggie want to stay on here? She was unnerved by what happened to Nell. So was I, but I had you. I think Maggie just wanted to get away from Raven Rock, as far away as possible!"

I was standing by a window where the noonday sun
poured hot and golden on my arm, yet I felt a bone-
deep chill, as if I had been standing in a snowstorm.

Twelve

Mrs. Edwin T. Prescott ("Call me Sadie!") was an alert, outspoken woman with ideas common to some of my own. I was astonished; I liked her! The routine meeting of the women's club provided a welcome lull in my emotional day. I nodded, smiled, and sipped as serenely as the most placid member, and almost deceived myself into believing the normalcy of my situation. Mrs. Prescott's witty and thoughtful comments during the interview made my job almost effortless. She was a reporter's delight, and the story had already taken form in my mind before I left the meeting.

Morgan Lawrence breezed past my cubbyhole as I finished typing the final draft, and I waved the copy to flag him down. He glanced at it hurriedly, then read it a second time.

"Good! Very good." He cocked his head. "Did you make this up, or was she really that interesting?"

"She was interesting," I confessed. "And contrary to popular belief, all women's club presidents don't have sagging bosoms."

He blushed. "Hmmm, maybe next time I should go myself." He paused on his way out. "Did Seth Honeycutt reach you? He called here this morning, and I told him to try the school." Try as he would, he couldn't keep the curiosity from his voice.

It was difficult not to smile. "Yes, I talked with him. He said his mother has agreed to rent Honeysuckle House. I'm supposed to go there after work."

Morgan glanced at his watch. "It's almost five. You can leave now if you'd like."

I covered my typewriter. "They don't expect me until five-thirty. I'd like to look up something first. Do you keep copies of *The Register* as far back as twenty-three years?"

"Sure. There are stacks of them in bound copies in the back room, if you can fight the dust." His eyes narrowed. "Why? Are you thinking of a nostalgia feature?"

"No, I'm just curious. It's something Joyce McDonald told me, about a girl who lived in Honeysuckle House. She was murdered by somebody called the Chuckler." I studied his expression. "Do you remember anything about that?"

He stood with his arms folded. "Twenty-three years ago I was seven years old, but I do remember when that happened, and I've heard Dad talk about it. They caught the guy—a tramp, I think—but not before he had killed several women." His green eyes glinted. "You're not afraid of living in Honeysuckle House, are you? After all, this happened years ago."

I stiffened. "Of course not! It's just that Joyce and Dan were talking about this girl, about what happened, and I wanted to find out more about it. Who knows? Maybe it would make a good feature." I flushed at my defensive tone.

Morgan had noticed it, too. He grinned. "Uh-huh. Well, I have to run. There's a Lions meeting tonight, and I barely have time to go home and change." He nodded toward the room behind us. "The back issues are in there if you still want to sec them. If you need any help, ask Charlie. He'll be here a while longer."

The advertising manager was in his office going over layouts for the next issue. I knew he was there before I looked. I could smell his foul cigar. The dead stump protruded from his mouth like a grotesque appendage.

"Charlie, why don't you light that thing or throw it away?" I leaned against the door frame, holding my nose.

His stubby face lit up in a smile. "Why, this is the only way I can keep the women away! If it weren't for my cigar, I wouldn't have a snowman's chance in hell!" He flexed a pica stick in strong fingers.

I laughed. "Morgan said you might help me find some back issues. I wanted to read about the Chuckler murders."

"The Chuckler murders? What would you be knowing about that?" Charlie's cigar sagged. "Why, you weren't no more than a handshake when that happened."

I told him about Seth's offer of Honeysuckle House and the McDonalds' conversation that afternoon. "It happened about twenty-three years ago, they said."

Charlie shook his head as he switched on the light in the small storage room. "That was bad business, those murders, happened not long after I started working here." He tugged at a musty volume. "We try to keep them in order," he said, "but they have a way of getting messed up." He grunted. "Here we are! I think this is the right year." He flipped through the yellowed pages. "The first girl was killed in the spring, biggest news story *The Register* ever had, or has had since." Charlie changed his cigar to the other side of his mouth. "Lunatic killed three girls, one after another, and tried to kill more! Plain crazy, or mean, or both. We had reporters here covering the story from all over the place, big-city reporters, too." He smoothed the pages with tobacco-stained fingers. "Put Raven Rock in the news in a bad way."

"But they did catch him, didn't they?" My eyes studied the headlines.

"Yeah, some tramp. People around here were relieved! You could almost see the fear slough off of them." Charlie lifted the clumsy book to a wide shelf and dusted off a stool. "Here you go. Make yourself comfortable. I'm gonna leave you to it and get on back to that layout. It's all in there."

"Thanks, Charlie." I climbed on the stool and wrapped my feet around the rungs. The headline sprang from the page in bold, black type:

LOCAL TEACHER FOUND MURDERED

I plunged into the story seeking mention of Maggie Grey, but found none.

The body of Nell Gordon, a high school math teacher, had been found in the pine woods behind an abandoned cotton gin the morning after her murder. She had last been seen alive at a little past ten the night before as she left the high school, where she taught adult math classes.

Two of her students told the police they had offered Miss Gordon a ride, but she had declined because it was such a pretty night. Her roommate (Maggie Grey?) had reported her missing when she hadn't arrived at home by 1:00 A.M. But her body was not discovered until early the next morning.

Nell Gordon had been strangled with her own scarf. She had not been sexually molested. A scrap of paper found under the body had been torn from the woman's notebook. On it the murderer had drawn a crude picture of a clown's face and had printed in block letters his soon-to-be-feared pseudonym, the Chuckler.

There was silence in the dim, stuffy room. I listened for the comforting squeak of Charlie's chair and sensed a strange, creeping fear, as if my spine were turning to ice. Then papers rattled in the adjoining office, a metal pica stick clicked against the wooden desk, and some of the chill went away, but not all of it.

Nell Gordon had been killed in April. *The Register* recorded no murder the week following her death, but there had been a frightening incident involving a young mother. Ann Taylor had waited until twilight to gather her laundry from the line. She had collected the dry diapers, folding them one by one, and was walking back to the house with the basket when she heard the voice, a faint, spine-tingling chuckle. The attacker was upon her almost before she knew he was there, a tall, shadowy form, who apparently had been watching from the wooded area behind the house.

Ann Taylor managed to utter an ear-splitting scream as the assailant twisted one of her baby's diapers around her throat. Her husband and two close neighbors rushed out to find her, frightened and shaken, but alive. The Chuckler had escaped. Although the police were summoned immediately, they could find no trace of the man.

A week later, Wilma Lou Tatum, a carhop at the local drive-in, was found beside the lake road, strangled with the belt from her uniform. Again the Chuckler had left his calling card—the clown's face and his printed signature—this time on the back of an order sheet from the drive-in. No one had seen the girl leave the restaurant the night before, and her mother had not missed her until the following morning. Wilma Lou was eighteen years old.

I jumped when Charlie appeared in the doorway. "You gonna be long?" he muttered.

I looked up, welcoming the sight of him, the smell of his dreadful cigar. "No, I'll be through in a little while."

He leaned on the door frame. "This is our square-dancing night, the wife's and mine, so I'm gonna have to leave you now." He frowned, sucking on his soggy cigar. "I wouldn't stay here long, Henrietta."

"Don't worry," I said. "I don't plan to."

I heard him open the back door. "Don't forget to lock up!" he called. "And turn out the lights." He was humming.

I found the next murder headline in a June issue. Loretta Eddington, a comparative newcomer to Raven Rock, was the oldest of the victims. The body of the thirty-three-year-old widow had been discovered in the back room of her dress shop in the downtown business district, strangled like the others, this time with binding twine. The Chuckler left his message on one of the sales slips.

Friends of the woman said that she had been an optimistic, confident person who functioned well in emergencies. But Mrs. Eddington made three mistakes: She had stayed late to take inventory; she had been alone; and she had opened her door to the murderer. When her unsuspecting sales staff entered the store the next morning, they found the back door unlocked.

A feature story in a later issue played up the town's rising fear.

Doors are locked and bolted. Young women
no longer go out after dark, and parents are

keeping their teenage daughters at home. The menacing threat of the phantom Chuckler looms over this once peaceful town whose citizens struggle to deal with the horror of the senseless murders here.

Three young women have been killed and another attacked since the unknown killer first struck in April. Friends and neighbors of the victims react with shock and outrage at the murders that have stunned this small community.

"I still can't believe it," said Robert Hoffman, whose dry cleaning establishment is adjacent to Loretta Eddington's dress shop. "Mrs. Eddington was always pleasant, a smile for everyone. Why would anyone want to do that to her?"

"They say it's someone right here in Raven Rock, maybe somebody we've known all our lives." Mrs. Hattie Baker hurriedly purchased groceries, while her husband waited in the car. "I never thought I'd be afraid to go out alone in my own hometown!"

Shirley Logan, 16, and her friend Mary Tate, 17, waited for Shirley's mother to pick them up at the local swimming pool. "Miss Gordon was my favorite teacher," Shirley said with tears in her eyes. "She gave me a lot of extra help. I'm not too good in math."

"And Wilma Lou [Tatum], we've known her all our lives," Mary added. "Why, she sat right next to me in world history! I wish they'd hurry and catch this guy. I'm scared to go anywhere anymore."

"We all are," Shirley added.

"I believe it's somebody from outside the town," said Mayor Warren Crutchfield, "and

73

I don't think it will be long before we have him safely behind bars. Meanwhile," he added, "I suggest everyone take extra precautions when going out at night, or, better still, stay at home."

There were numerous follow-up stories about the investigation and articles on the possible identity of the Chuckler, but no reports of more attacks until July, when the Chuckler came out of hiding.

Ellen Rayfield, a twelve-year-old girl, had been attacked while on her way home from a church picnic on the evening of the Fourth of July.

The church was only two blocks from her home, and she had walked part of the way with friends. The man waylaid her at a vacant lot within sight of her home, while it was still light. Her screams aroused neighbors, who found her, dazed and bruised, behind an abandoned garage. The girl's undergarments had been removed, but she was not raped.

Ellen told police that the man grabbed her through an opening in the fence and clamped one hand over her mouth as she walked past. Her struggling forced his hand to slip long enough for the girl to scream for help. He then struck her with a piece of wood, and she lost consciousness. The man was tall, unshaven, and dirty, the child said, adding that he had reeked of a sickening, sour smell. About a fourth of a bottle of cheap whiskey had been found on the site. The attacker did not wear a clown's mask, but as she lost consciousness, Ellen said, she thought she heard him chuckling.

Following issues of *The Register* were filled with stories on the subsequent capture of the man, a vagabond, whom Ellen Rayfield identified as her attacker. The tramp had been living in the old cotton gin where the first victim was found.

Among his possessions were clippings of the murders, an advertisement for a circus featuring a clown's face, and a silver charm bracelet that had belonged to Wilma Lou Tatum. The Chuckler had finally been stopped.

I let out a slow, uneasy breath in the well-deep silence of the room. It was almost six o'clock, and I had told the Honeycutts I would drop by at five-thirty. My eyes were burning from reading in the poor light, and my shoulders ached. I stretched and climbed stiffly from the stool, leaving the bound issues on the shelf.

The pressroom was dark, the hulking silhouette of the huge old press ominous in the gloom. The front office was empty. I would have welcomed even the smacking of Mildred's constant chewing, but Mildred was gone. I had left a light burning over my desk and hurried toward its brightness to grab my pocketbook and leave. Outside the day had turned dreary, and I didn't want to get caught in a storm. I glimpsed my disheveled hair in one of the framed editions that lined the walls and wondered if I should take time to comb it before I left. I had decided not to bother when the knob turned on the front door of the office. The shade flapped as it opened, and someone stepped inside. The filing cabinet blocked my view, and I took refuge in its shadow, gripping my pocketbook as if it were a weapon. The gate to the front section squeaked open . . .

"Henrietta? Anybody there?"

It was Seth Honeycutt! I peeked around my hiding place at his puzzled face. "Over here!" I called. "I was just leaving." I hoped he couldn't hear my heart; it couldn't seem to stop its drumroll.

"I had to run by the store for Mother, and I thought you might have forgotten what time it was. Oh, and we'd like you to stay for supper, if you don't mind cold cuts." He stepped into my tiny office area. "Why on earth were you hiding back here?"

"I wasn't hiding, I was just . . ." I laughed. "Well, I was hiding, I guess. I had been reading some crazy, creepy stories when I heard the front door open. I didn't know who it was."

He grinned. "You must have been raised in a city. Nobody locks doors in Raven Rock."

"Just the same, I'd appreciate it if you'd stick around while I lock up," I said. It surprised me how much people could forget in twenty-three years.

Thirteen

Honeysuckle House both attracted and repelled me. I felt an odd sense of acceptance there, as if I were coming home. Yet there was an element I couldn't pinpoint, a veiled feeling of apprehension that made me want to look over my shoulder.

The cottage was dark the afternoon I first went inside with Essie and Seth. The electricity had not been turned on, and it had begun to rain. The enclosing trees and vines allowed a minimum of gray light inside, adding to the drab effect.

Yet in spite of the gloomy interior, I could envision a sunny transformation, a place of belonging, where my mother once had lived.

It was because my mother *had* lived in Honeysuckle House that I had agreed to stay, that and my liking for Essie and Seth, who were becoming like a family to me. I trailed after them that day through the small, two-story house, peeking into dusty corners, probing cobwebby closets with the flashlight's beam. In spite of the dank smell of the place, I whiffed an elusive fragrance, something light and airy that reminded me of spring. I ran a finger along the rough, peeling paint

77

of an upstairs wall. These rooms, familiar to my mother, would become familiar to me. Here, perhaps I could piece together the puzzle of her disappearance.

Bits of information had accumulated in my mind, facts I had acquired about Margaret Grey. They had no anchor, fit no plan. I needed the time and the quietude to weave them into a sensible foundation. Only then could I proceed to unravel the mystery of Maggie Grey. Already I knew the name of the town where my grandparents lived—Shannon. I wanted to abandon everything, my job, the school, the cottage, and rush to the place where I was almost certain to find kin. But Shannon was over 200 miles away; I had measured the distance on my road map. It would endanger my position in Raven Rock if I left, even for a day. It was too soon, and when I did go, I must have a reason, a good one. I had taken advantage of the public telephone in town to call the Shannon exchange. The operator had given me two listings, one for a Warren J. Grey and another for an H.D. Grey. Surely one of them would hold a clue to the secret of my identity. I relished the confidence of that knowledge, tucked it away to savor at my will, like a secret treasure. Meanwhile, I occupied myself with readying Honeysuckle House.

In the days that followed, an area was cleared around the cottage and some of the vines torn away. Sunlight reclaimed Honeysuckle House. The house clamored with the sounds of workmen as repairs were made, plumbing patched, and a new sink installed in the kitchen. Essie had the house rewired and bought a used stove and refrigerator to replace the old ones.

The house had two bedrooms over a living room, kitchen, and bath. If I had had to paint the big, high-ceilinged rooms alone, I don't think I would ever have finished. But Joyce and Dan McDonald made good on their offer to help, and since Seth was remodeling the kitchen, I'm afraid he got swept up in the arrangement. (I think he was afraid we would track paint over his new linoleum.) I was surprised when Morgan approached me the Friday before we were to begin.

"What time does the party start?" He had just completed his column for the next week's edition and was rewarding himself with a pack of cheese crackers. The crumbs sifted onto my desk.

"What party?" I was in good humor because he had asked me to cover city court the day before, and even his messy eating habits didn't irritate me.

"The painting party!" He offered a cracker. "Aren't you planning on sprucing up Essie's cottage this weekend?"

"Well, sure, anytime tonight after supper. Are you offering your assistance?"

He tossed the cellophane wrapper at my trash can and missed. "Are you offering your beer?"

"The refrigerator is full," I said. "Just bring your paintbrush!"

With so many helpers, I was afraid we would get in one another's way, and I was right. But everyone was in a festive mood, and we managed to make some sort of progress without treading too heavily on each other's feet and nerves.

The dreary, barren living room took on new life with the clutter of paint cans, ladders, and brushes, the banter of helpful friends. It was a good beginning.

Joyce McDonald dipped her brush into the spattered can. "This color, it's almost identical to the shade of yellow the walls used to be." She stared at the dingy plaster. "How could you tell?"

I hitched up the strap of my overalls. "I couldn't. I just guessed. Honeysuckle House should have pale yellow walls to go with its name. Besides, yellow is one of my favorite colors." I eased my brush carefully down the window trim. "It's funny, but this house even smells like honeysuckle to me."

Morgan moved the stepladder to a corner of the room, almost tripping over the drop cloth. "You have a good imagination. All I can smell is paint."

Dan looked at me curiously over his paint tray. "Oh, come on now, Henri! Honeysuckle isn't even blooming."

"But I do smell it!" I protested. "I smelled it as soon as I came in the door. It's faint, but it's there, especially in that room upstairs, the one over the kitchen."

Joyce crouched over the baseboard, a streak of yellow across her cheek. "That's funny . . ." She looked at Dan.

"What?" I wiped a smear from the window glass.

She shrugged. "Funny that you should smell honeysuckle when it's not in bloom."

I knew she was lying. "That's not what you meant. Why won't you tell me?"

Joyce concentrated on her baseboard. "I'll tell you after you bribe me with beer."

She was trying to pass it off lightly, but I intended to get to the bottom of it. I was going to pursue the matter when the doorbell rang. Seth ran from the kitchen where he had been sanding the cabinets. "I'll get it! I don't have paint on my hands." He swung open the door. "Well, guess who's here to help?"

"Help, nothin'! Where's the beer?" Pat Saxon, in paint-splotched jeans and shirt, waved a paint roller over her head. "I'll do anything but windows!"

80

Seth grinned. "Where's your other half?"

"Are you kidding? I can't even get him to paint his own house. Besides, somebody has to babysit." Pat's gaze wandered over the room. "I've always wondered what this place looked like inside. It's going to be pretty, Henri. I like it."

I laughed. "It beats the Raven Rock Motel! And after we paint over the grime, it might just look like home."

But painting over the grime took longer than I expected, even with six of us working. And after four hours of continuous painting, we collapsed on sticky newspapers on the living-room floor and admired our accomplishments.

Hands over his eyes, Morgan inspected the dazzling red and yellow kitchen. "Can you imagine having to look at this with a hangover?"

"I don't intend to have a hangover," I said, thirstily turning up a can of beer, "except, maybe tomorrow!"

"I wish Seth would hurry with those hamburgers!" Pat's stomach growled. "I didn't know I could work up such an appetite."

"He only volunteered to go so he could get out of painting," Dan complained. "Wish I'd thought of it first."

Joyce raised her beer. "Let's drink a toast to Henri in her new house! How are you going to furnish it, Henri?"

"There's some furniture in the attic here that Essie says is mostly junk, but there are a couple of good wicker chairs and an old oak daybed. Wait until you see that daybed! It's from the Jacobean period, I think. I can just see it covered in turquoise, a deep turquoise. Wouldn't that be pretty with draperies in a yellow and turquoise print, and braided rugs?" I rambled on about my decorating intentions while Pat nodded in agreement. "And bookshelves," I went on. "Bookshelves on either side of the fireplace, like it was before . . ."

My rambling broke off as suddenly as it began, the words crumbling into silence.

Both hands gripping the ladder, Joyce stared down at me. "How did you know how it was before?"

"Why, I guess you told me."

She shook her head. "No, I don't think I did."

I shrugged. "Then it must have been Essie or Seth."

Pat's down-to-earth voice brought us back to reality. "What difference does it make where she got her ideas? Turquoise is a natural choice for yellow; I'd pick it myself. And this room calls for braided rugs. Can you imagine using anything else?"

"I'm sorry. I'm being silly, I guess." Joyce's usually hearty voice was no more than a whisper. "I just felt funny all of a sudden, like a rabbit ran over my grave."

"Blame it on hunger," Dan said, crossing to the window. "Ahh!" He rubbed his hands together. "We feast at last! Here comes Seth with the food."

When I had finished my burger, I turned to Joyce, who stood silently by the ladder contemplating the foam on her beer. "Tell me what it was like living here," I said.

She took a long, slow swallow, pausing before she answered. "It was fun, almost like being in college, except we were working girls. Nell was kind of quiet, but nice, the studious type. She read a lot, played chess." Joyce smiled. "I guess Nell was the brainy one."

"And the other girl? Maggie . . . what was her name?" I tried to control the quiver in my voice.

Joyce stared at her reflection in the dark window. "Maggie Grey. Maggie was an elf, always laughing. We had a lot of fun together." She glanced at Dan. "We weren't too terribly sophisticated, were we? And Maggie liked to experiment in the kitchen. When I think of some of the concoctions she turned out. Ugh! But she was a kindhearted person, impulsive maybe, but kindhearted. I remember how she used to help her home economics students with their sewing projects after school. Nell and I learned not to walk into the living room, ever, without looking for patterns and materials spread all over the floor." She smiled. "Not many teachers care enough to do things like that, but Maggie really liked those kids."

Morgan opened another beer. "I can't seem to picture Nell, but I remember Maggie. She was special."

Dan looked at his watch. "I hate to break up the party, but my back is crying for a hot tub."

Joyce made a face. "You just won't let anybody forget our ages, will you?" She paused as I was walking them to the door. "Another thing about Maggie," she said. "That honeysuckle smell you mentioned, it was her favorite scent. She never wore anything else."

Fourteen

I moved into Honeysuckle House the last week in September. I had been living my "other life" in Raven Rock for a little over a month. I call it that because there was an unreal, charadelike quality about my existence there. The Henrietta Meredith who worked for *The Register,* taught journalism at the Raven Rock School and had no relationship with the girl who had been at the university. I was a character in a play with the town as my stage. It was a treacherous role. Sometimes I longed for the other me, the happy, complacent me from another time, another place. Sometimes I had trouble keeping the two apart.

The cottage was clean, bright, and bare, empty of furniture except for the few pieces I had resurrected from Essie's attic. Pat Saxon's mother had agreed to make slipcovers for the chairs and daybed, and draperies for the living-room windows, but it would be weeks before she finished. I had purchased a bright braided rug and two bookcases from a local furniture store, and that, with an old enamel kitchen table and two straight chairs (also from the attic), comprised my furnishings for the house. I slept on the daybed in the living room, using my suitcase as a dresser until I could arrange for Emmett to ship some of the things I had stored above his shop. I thought longingly of the warm maple bedroom suite Dad had given me on my thirteenth birthday. It would look attractive in one of the rooms upstairs. Mom's cherry desk and a few other occasional pieces would help to fill in the spaces in the large living room. I would tie my two selves together with belongings, part of the old, part of the new. I looked forward to seeing Emmett again, selecting the furniture to be sent. Also, it would give me an excuse to get away. I planned to combine that trip with a visit to Shannon to seek out my grandparents. I could do it over a weekend and would have a perfectly legitimate reason for leaving if anyone asked.

My outlook was more positive than it had been in months. More than anything else, my part-time position as a journalism instructor had helped me peel off some of my shell of self-concern. Since the news of my adoption I had unconsciously burrowed deeper and deeper into my own problems, lost myself in the quest for my origin. I had forgotten how to live.

Kids won't stand for that. After our first classroom session, I realized I had just spent fifty minutes without thinking of myself. It was as if someone had opened a window in a stuffy room. And the prodigious creation of that first smudged copy of the school newspaper (titled "What's Happening" by popular ballot) awakened in me an enthusiasm that had been dulled by four years of college sophistication.

Our star reporter was Pat Saxon's fifth-grader Mary Faye, who turned out copy as clean and uncluttered as her fresh, bright face and neat, brown hair. Her best friend Hannah Whitaker made up for Mary Faye's lack of adjectives. Description just came naturally to

Hannah. She had words enough to go around and then some, as illustrated by the first news story she submitted:

Dr. Lawrence Speaks
to Mrs. Cooper's Class

Dr. Lawrence told us all about being a doctor last week. Some of the things he said were funny and some were sad. Dr. Lawrence is old, but he doesn't look it, even if he does have white hair. He's a nice man who has helped a lot of people. I like him. I've known him all my life.

I showed the story to Joyce as we were eating lunch in the cafeteria. "What in the world am I going to do with this?"

Joyce chuckled as she read it. "Pity you have to change it. She has him down pat."

I stirred the thick, meaty soup and watched the steam swirl into my face. "Dr. Lawrence? Isn't that Morgan's father?"

Joyce nodded. "Yes, and he's all those things Hannah says he is." She laughed. "You're going to love Hannah, but you'll never make a reporter out of her."

She was right. The next time the class met, I called Hannah aside to discuss her article, pointing out the errors.

She rolled her large, gray eyes to the ceiling, flipped back her thick, yellow braids. "But I *like* to describe things! I like to write interesting stories." She looked down at her toes, wiggled them in shabby, brown sandals. "Writing news stories doesn't sound like much fun!"

We compromised. Hannah rewrote her story about Dr. Lawrence to suit my requirements, and I assigned her a feature article on Honey Bear, the lovable, brown mongrel who had become the school's mascot.

Still, I worried about Hannah. Unlike her jean-clad classmates, she always came to school in a dress. She reminded me of a pioneer child in her crisp cottons. She and Mary Faye seemed devoted to one another and presented a contrast in coloring and personality: sensible Mary Faye, dark-haired and slender; Hannah the dreamer, fair and chunky. They sat together in class, ate together, played together. Joyce said it had always been that way. They seemed contented in their friendship, yet there was a quality about Hannah Whitaker that bothered me, a pathetic quality that slowly revealed itself through my association with the child.

"She has a tough time at home," Joyce explained when I asked her about it. "Her father is a strict, religious man, and her brothers and sisters are all older than she is. She's the last one at home."

"What about her mother?" I pictured Hannah's mother as a large, happy woman with her hair in a bun; someone who baked a lot.

"She's nice. Ruth Whitaker's a fine woman. She's just worn out. She raised all her kids, and then this one came along." Joyce sighed. "Ruth and her husband both work at the mill. They don't have much, but they get by. I think he's the problem. I expect things are pretty drab at home for Hannah. That's probably why she likes to make up stories."

"She always wears dresses," I pointed out. "I know she must feel out of place."

Joyce frowned. "That's her father again. Luke Whitaker's a strange man, unforgiving. One of their girls, the oldest, I think, got pregnant before she married. It happens in the best of families, and she did marry the man, but Luke won't have anything to do with her. And it's been several years now. He's so afraid poor little Hannah is going to do something sinful, he won't even let her wear pants, won't let her do much of anything the other kids do."

I shook my head. "That's a shame. She's a sweet child, and bright. She should be having fun."

Joyce smiled at me in a strange way. "I'm glad to hear you're concerned."

I watched her face. "Maybe it's my imagination, but I don't like the way you're looking at me."

"You're an outdoor person," Joyce continued. "I know you like to bike." She smiled. "I'll bet you like hiking, too, don't you? And camping out under the stars, telling ghost stories, eating burned marshmallows?"

I backed away. "What are you getting at?"

"Well, you do, don't you?" She folded her arms, tapped a foot.

"So what if I do?"

"I knew it!" Joyce laughed, clapping her stubby hands together. "Dan and I have this little custom, you see. Nothing organized, but we've been doing it for several years now."

I frowned. "Doing what?"

"Oh, camping, hiking, the usual outdoor stuff." Her face grew serious. "Some of these kids, Hannah, for instance, don't get much of a chance to do things like that. So, a few years ago, Dan and I decided to ask a few to come with us. Our kids were grown, and we missed having them along. Now it's become a tradition. We plan hikes once in a while, picnics, things kids like to do. And once or twice a year we take them camping."

I laughed. "You must be a glutton for punishment!"

"Not really. We just pick up and go when the mood strikes us, and if the kids want to come along, that's fine." She smiled. "And they usually do. It's good for them and for us. You'll enjoy it too, Henri."

"Well . . ." I couldn't think of an excuse.

"We're thinking of a bike hike in a week or so," Joyce went on. She closed her eyes. "Just think of it, crisp, autumn leaves, the wind in your face, the smell of wood smoke . . ."

"Okay, okay!" I laughed. "I'm sold! You can stop now. Just give me a chance to get settled. I have to make a trip to pick up some furniture next weekend. After that, maybe I can."

"Good! We'll count on you. Oh, and tell Morgan to plan on coming too, will you?"

"Morgan?"

Joyce nodded. "Sure. He usually likes to come along, if he isn't off chasing some girl."

I wondered how Morgan and I would get along together on an outdoor excursion. He had seemed friendly enough while we were painting Honeysuckle House, and we were compatible at the office, or had been until I suggested remodeling *The Register*'s working area.

"Do *what?*" He had thundered. "What's wrong with it the way it is?"

"It's cramped, for one thing," I explained. "And it's dusty, dirty, and altogether grim."

Morgan's face was grim, too. His mouth drew into a tight line, but I rambled on.

"It makes me sneeze," I said. "And these partitions, they're like cages. They give me claustrophobia."

"If the dust bothers you, clean it up," he snorted. "And as for those partitions, they've been here as long as I can remember. They've never bothered anyone else."

I moved a step closer. "If God had intended for man to fly, he would have given him wings."

His brows went up. "What?"

"In other words," I said, "what was good enough for great-grandpa is good enough for you."

He turned and walked away, his face mottled. "Women!" he muttered. "Give them a little responsibility, and they want to change the world!" He roamed through the office, grumbling about interfering people who liked to spend someone else's money and scraped his shin on a corner of one of his precious railings.

I smiled about it for the rest of the day.

Fifteen

It was lonely at Honeysuckle House. The days had grown shorter, and the deep, gray twilight outside my window connected shadows until everything was dark. From my living room I watched the yellow squares of light from Essie's windows across the lawn and felt a pang of regret for not accepting her invitation for dinner. I had dined with them often in the past weeks and had begun to depend on her warm company and home-cooked meals. It was time, I thought, that I became adjusted to living alone.

I pulled the shades on my long windows, shutting out the cozy picture. The boarders would be settling in the comfortable living room, the Waverly sisters to continue their endless bickering, the others to read or watch television. Essie would be stacking the huge dishwasher, sloshing pans in mounds of suds: homey, busy, everyday things that other people did. I brought my sandwich and apple into the living room where I curled up on my new rug with the torrid novel Pat had said would singe the pinfeathers off a chicken. But the sandwich lay untouched on my plate, and the book remained open to page one. My supper did not appeal to me, nor did the erotic details of someone else's love life.

I sat in the quiet house listening to the faint hum of the refrigerator, the occasional stir of traffic in the street, and tried to remember my mother's face in the missing photograph, reconstruct her personality.

It was obvious that she had been beautiful, had enjoyed cooking and sewing, was fond of working with young people. These facts were known to her most casual acquaintances. She had been kindhearted, Joyce had said. Perhaps too kindhearted? But what was Maggie Grey really like? Did she have a sense of humor? Believe in God? Like animals? Did she prefer sweet pickles to sour?

The Chuckler murders had frightened her, naturally. She had lost a good friend, a roommate. She was alone and pregnant and unmarried; it was not, at that time, an acceptable state. But why run away? She had friends here, relatives in Shannon, I presumed.

I reexamined my information on the murders, tried to determine what the victims had in common with Maggie Grey. The first one was obvious. Nell Gordon had been her roommate and a teacher in the same school. Wilma Lou Tatum, the teenage carhop, might have been one of her students. But the widowed dress shop owner apparently had no connection, nor did the young mother who had luckily escaped. The child, the last person who had been attacked, was grown now and married, Joyce had said. She lived in another state. Ann Taylor, the only other victim to escape, moved away soon after the attack. There was nothing to go on except old newspapers, gossip, and instinct.

I bit absently into my apple. Friday, I thought, Friday I'll know more about Maggie Grey. But would Friday ever, ever come?

A rustling of leaves outside the cottage startled me. I crouched there, unmoving, as someone stepped up to the door.

"Henri? Henri, are you there? I have a surprise for you."

My fear melted at the sound of Seth's voice, and I hurried to open the door. He stood in the pale square of light with a shoe box in one hand and a foil-wrapped package in the other. I saw him glance at my meager supper. "Good! I see you haven't eaten. Here." He pushed the warm, foil bundle into my hands. "This place is too lonely," he said, looking around at my bare room. "It's like a tomb in here." He smiled. "I've brought you a roommate."

I eagerly unwrapped the foil bundle. "Fried chicken?"

"The chicken's for your supper, silly!" He held out the shoe box. "Here's your surprise."

I lifted the top and scooped up the tiny scrap of kitten, nuzzling it under my chin.

"Every old maid should have one." Seth grinned.

"He's adorable! Where did you find him?" I stroked the soft, white fur.

"It's a *she*, I'm afraid." He stood back, watching me, a slight smile on his lips. "I found it in a cotton patch."

I moved to the kitchen, snatched a carton of milk from the refrigerator. Seth and I sat at my kitchen table as we waited for the milk to warm. "Are you sure it doesn't belong to somebody?" I asked. "What was it doing in a cotton patch? What were *you* doing in a cotton patch?"

"It was hiding under the steps of this little country store where I stopped for a soft drink this afternoon," he explained. "A dog had chased it out of a cotton patch behind the store. Poor little thing was scared to

93

death. The storekeeper was delighted to have me take it off his hands."

The kitten licked her paws and stalked the kitchen, her tail like an exclamation mark. Seth grinned. "A country kitten for a city girl! How do you like your new roommate?"

I had already started making a bed for my pet, padding a box with an old towel. "I'll call her Cotton," I said. "And we'll get along fine. There's only one thing," I added, "I'm afraid you, or somebody, will have to kitten-sit this weekend. I'm going to be out of town."

He drummed his fingers on the table. "I'll be at a convention this weekend, but I'm sure Mother . . ."

"No!" I protested louder than I had intended. "I'm sorry. I didn't mean to yell. It's just that I don't want to take advantage of your mother's good nature. She's done so much already."

His dark eyes were soft with concern. "Mother wouldn't want you to feel that way, Henri. She enjoys having you here." He paused, waiting for me to say something.

I rested my hand on his arm. "I think I know the very person to fill in for the weekend, Pat's daughter, Mary Faye! She'd love taking care of Cotton. I just might have trouble getting her back."

I followed him to the door, and both of us were careful where we put our feet. He hesitated before leaving and gave my hand a squeeze. "Be careful, Henrietta, wherever you're going."

"I will. You too, Seth. And thanks for bringing Cotton. It will be nice to have someone to come home to."

I remembered Seth's voice as I drove toward Shannon that Friday afternoon. "Be careful, wherever you're going." Why had he said it like that? What did he mean? He knew I was going to get my furniture out of storage; everyone did. Did he guess that I had another mission?

I pushed down on the accelerator, as if I could leave my suspicions behind. I had left the office at four, packed and ready, and was hoping to reach Shannon by eight. There was no motel in the small village, but I had arranged for accommodations at a Howard Johnson's in a town not twenty miles away.

Brilliant autumn scenery flashed by me as the mountain road unfolded. The vibrant reds of dogwood and sumac, always the first to turn; the throbbing gold of hickory; the brown stubble of a hayfield in the dying sun. I drove past skeletons of cornstalks, orange pumpkins scattered against the russet earth. A picture of a peaceful harvest, the serene landscape calmed me, reminded me of Thanksgiving: warm fires, good smells, and home. Would Shannon be like that? Shannon was probably as close to home as I was going to get.

Oddly, the closer I got to Shannon, the more relaxed I became. I found myself looking forward to the bike hike with Joyce and Dan, hoping for good weather. I smiled, thinking of Cotton, who would be spending the next two nights next to Mary Faye's bed. She would probably be spoiled rotten when I came to collect her on Sunday, but how nice it would be to have another living, breathing creature in Honeysuckle House.

I stopped at a hamburger place about sixty miles from my destination and was surprised at how hungry I had become. An hour later in my hotel room, I sat by the telephone, my calmness gone. The two Greys were listed in the phone book. Should I call first? What would I say? In my rush to get there, even during the long drive when I had had time to think, I had never considered a suitable story to explain my presence there.

Both families were listed with a route number; there was no street address. How could I possibly find them unless I telephoned first? I had no choice. I dialed the first listing, my breath coming in short, fast gasps. I couldn't seem to get enough air. A man answered. His voice had a country twang. Gulping, I explained that my mother had been a Grey whose relatives had come from that area and I was working on a family history.

"How long ago did they live here?" he drawled.

"At least twenty-three years," I said. "Probably longer."

"Couldn't be us, then. We only come here five year ago." I heard someone say something in the background. "My wife says it's been six," he added. "But that still don't help you none, does it?"

Disappointment welled within me. "No, I guess it doesn't."

"You might try that other Grey. She's not kin to us, been here a lot longer than we have, too. Might be the one you want."

It has to be, I thought. Oh, please! It just has to be! I forced myself to wait before calling the next number, rehearsing my speech in my mind. It occurred to me that the remaining Grey might not want to see me, even if we were related, might not even believe me. Country people are wary of strangers.

An emptiness consumed me as the phone rang. I steeled myself against disappointment. A tired-voiced woman finally answered, and I repeated my story.

There was a long pause. I was afraid she was going to hang up on me. "Please," I said. "This is so important to me! I don't know anyone else to ask."

"Well, my husband's family has lived around here for as long as I can remember," she said. "But they're all gone now. I'm the last one by that name." Her words were bleak, lonely, as if she were the last person in the world.

"I'm sorry," I said. "I think I know how you must feel. My people are gone, too."

"What did you say your name was?" The question came in a whisper.

"Henrietta Meredith," I said. And please don't hang up! I begged silently.

"And where are you calling from?"

I told her.

"If you'd like to come by, I can give you directions, or perhaps I could meet you somewhere." Her murmured words ran together.

"No, I can drive there, be there in about twenty minutes." I looked at my watch. It was almost nine. "Is it all right to come out tonight, or would you rather I wait until morning?"

"Oh, come tonight." She paused. "That is, if it's convenient."

"I was hoping you'd say that. Now, tell me how to get there."

Sixteen

The modest farmhouse sat back from the main road at the end of a straight, narrow driveway. Although it was probably built in the Victorian era, it was functional and uncluttered, softened only by a lacework of vines across the porch. As I drove nearer, I could see that someone had attempted to brighten it with yellow paint.

The night closed in like two black walls on either side of the gravel road. I was in a one-way tunnel with the house at the end. A small woman waited in the yellow light of the porch, hugging a sweater around her. In the light her hair looked yellow, too, but I saw that it was not. It was gray, and she was old. She didn't look anything like my mother's picture. She didn't look anything like me.

I stepped out of the car like someone in slow motion, and she moved imperceptibly to meet me. She made no move to touch me, but turned at the bottom of the steps. "Come in." Her face was in shadow, her voice a monotone. She could be anyone's mother, or no one's. She could be a lonely old woman in need of companionship.

In the living room, green upholstered furniture faced a television set across a flowered carpet. Crocheted doilies protected the backs and arms of the chairs. The room was worn and faded, but respectable. It had a forgotten smell of old books no longer read, hearth fires no longer lit. On the mantel a Seth Thomas clock ticked away the years.

I waited for her to ask me to sit down and moved uneasily to the center of the room. From an upright piano in a dark corner, my mother's picture smiled at me. It was the same picture I had seen in Essie's annual.

I don't remember walking across the room, picking it up. I was standing there, holding it, my fingers caressing the tarnished metal frame, when I sensed her waiting behind me.

"You knew her?" There was an undercurrent of urgency in her voice.

"Yes. No! I . . . I don't remember her. I don't remember her at all!" Tears choked my words, and I sat on the arm of the overstuffed chair and buried my face in the back of it.

She let me cry, never speaking, never moving until I was done. Then she touched my arm, lightly, patiently, "Henrietta?"

I looked at her old face with the tears inching down it: dark eyes behind bifocals, hair that had once been brown. She seemed to be studying my face. "My name is Henrietta, too."

The picture still smiled up at us from where I clutched it in my lap. "Was she . . . ?"

"My daughter." She took the picture from me, polished the glass with her sweater, replaced it on the piano. "Do you know where she is? You must tell me, please! Where is my Maggie?"

I shook my head. "I don't know. I want to find her, too." I held out my hands to her. "She was my mother."

She nodded, still crying, her cool, dry hands grasping mine. "I know. I knew it when I saw you, but I was afraid to hope. There's not much hope left in me. I used it up long ago." She smiled for the first time. "You're very much like her, you know."

We sipped wine, homemade muscadine brought up from the cellar, sweet and musty, and sat, one on either side of the oilcloth-covered kitchen table with a freshly baked pound cake between us. It was a beautiful, golden cake, but neither of us touched it. I told her my story, beginning with the news of Mom's illness, and she told me hers.

Maggie had come to her father in September before she left Raven Rock, had come to him for help. She was frightened and pregnant, and he had turned her away.

My grandmother twisted a button on her sweater. "If only I had been here! But I was away, you see. One of our neighbors had died, and there were all those people to see to. I stayed all day." She cut another slice of the cake, although there were more than enough slices still undisturbed. "He told me about it when I got home, told me what he'd done.

" 'Why didn't you wait for me, call me?' I asked him. 'Why did you send her away?' And do you know what he said?"

She didn't wait for my reply. "Said he'd told her not to shame me any more than she already had, told Maggie not to bother me—me, her own mother! He'd wanted to spare me, he said. *Spare* me! I hated my husband for that, my own husband."

"Did you get in touch with her then?" I swirled the wine in my glass, hypnotized by its deep, red lights.

100

"I never saw my daughter again," she said. "Oh, I called that place where she stayed, talked with that woman, Mrs. Honeycutt, but Maggie never came back to Raven Rock.

"Milton—that's my husband, your grandfather—he was a strict unbending man. Oh, he was a good man, and he loved Maggie, but he loved her in his own way." She lifted her eyes to mine. "It wasn't enough."

"I'm sure he must have regretted . . ." I began.

"Oh, he did, he did. The guilt of it just about killed him, did kill him in a way. He died of a heart attack less than a year after that. It broke his heart that Maggie would go and do a thing like that, and he lashed out the only way he knew how. He regretted it, but he regretted it too late." She lifted a piece of cake to a plate and put it in front of me. I nibbled at the crust.

"We tried to find her," she went on. "I don't know how many times we made the trip to Raven Rock. Nobody knew where she went, nobody." She sighed. "After Milton died, I almost gave up hoping. Maggie was the only child we ever had, and I didn't know where she was!" She smiled. "But I knew that somewhere I had a grandchild, Maggie's child. And that's what kept me going."

I broke off another bite of cake. It tasted like nutmeg. "Do you know, did my mother say who my father was?"

She shook her head. "If only she had! If we had known that, we might have been able to find her. I hoped, we both hoped, she would marry the man, but now of course, I know she didn't."

"There's something wrong," I said. "Something missing. She wouldn't just disappear."

"She's dead, Henrietta. Your mother's dead. My daughter's dead. Accept it. I know my daughter. Maggie would never have left her baby to be raised by someone else, not if she had a choice."

"I intend to find out what happened, why she was so afraid." I drained the wine from my glass. The warm liquid gave me false courage, but it was better than no courage at all. "If I have to live in Raven Rock for the rest of my life, I'll find out what happened to my mother!"

"No!" It was the first time she had raised her voice. "You're young. You have your own life to live. Maggie's dead, and we can't bring her back." She stood behind my chair, put her soft cheek next to mine. "You're all I have, Henrietta. You're all that matters now."

It had seemed so long since anyone fussed over me, loved me enough to care, that I was tempted to agree with her, give up my search for Maggie Grey. After all, if she was dead, what good could it possibly do her? If she wasn't, she definitely didn't want us to know of her existence. But I knew I was fooling myself. I had no intentions of giving up. It was too late to turn back now. I covered her hand with mine. "I'll be all right," I insisted. "What could possibly happen to me in a little place like Raven Rock?"

"What happened to those other women, Henrietta? What happened to your mother?" Her words were stark. "Don't you understand, child? If your mother had enemies in Raven Rock, you could have enemies there, too."

"But they don't even know who I am," I explained. "No one in Raven Rock knows Maggie Grey was my mother."

"I knew," my grandmother said. "I took one look at you and knew."

I put my arms around her. The top of her head came to my chin. "It's been over twenty years," I said. "Those people barely remember her. It's different with you. Grandmother?" The name came easily, as if it had been waiting to be spoken. "You're going to have to keep our secret for a while, just until I work things out. No one must know who I am, who my mother was, not yet."

She moved around the kitchen, puttering about the stove, touching the glossy leaves of a plant in the window. "When . . . will I see you again?"

"Of course you will, and soon! I'll visit in a few weeks, and I'll call often, but no one must know. If anyone asks, tell them I'm a niece, a cousin, anybody, just for a while."

She smiled. "But we know better, don't we?"

I looked around at my grandmother's big, high-ceilinged kitchen: the worn linoleum; the red-and-white oilcloth; the wine that smelled of sweet summer; the little figure in the sweater who had just lost ten years off her face. I had never had a grandmother before. I helped myself to another piece of cake and laughed. "We certainly do know better," I said.

Seventeen

That night I had a dream. I was in a garden, a strange garden filled with vivid turquoise flowers I had never seen before. The scent of honeysuckle was heavy around me, and the air hummed with the sound of bees. A girl waited on a stone bench at the end of the path. It was my mother, young, smiling. She seemed to be expecting me and stood when she saw me.

Then it seemed as if she looked right through me, for as I drew nearer, she turned and picked up a pair of garden shears lying on the bench beside her and began to clip the thin, green stems. As she cut into one, blood ran over her hand, thick, bright blood as red as wine . . .

I sat up in bed in my motel room and looked at my watch. It was not yet five o'clock, and I was not due at my grandmother's for breakfast until eight. I watched the gray slit of dawn slip through my draperies, listened as the few early travelers loaded their cars and drove away. Daylight was a long time in coming.

I didn't mention the dream to my grandmother. I had already alarmed her enough. We had visited late the night before, and even after I returned to the motel, it seemed like hours before I went to sleep. It wasn't surprising that the excitement and the wine had created insomnia and nightmares.

From Shannon I drove to the city I once called home, arriving there in midafternoon. Seeing Emmett and the bakery was almost like coming home. He was shorthanded, as usual, so I accepted an apron and waited on customers out front. Mom's absence in the shop was a deep void that no one could fill. I missed her bustling presence, her cheerful voice. But it was good to be occupied, exchange news with Emmett, see familiar faces once again.

I selected the furniture for Honeysuckle House and made arrangements to have it delivered the next week. That night I stayed with an old school friend—the last of the old maids, we called ourselves—and she laughed when I told her about the cat. The two of us chatted like teenagers far into the night, and I found I hadn't forgotten how to giggle. It was a brief but relaxing visit, and I thought of it with pleasure during the drive back to Raven Rock. I had told Emmett of my mother's having lived there, but said nothing of the murders or of my grandmother's identity. There would be time for that after I discovered the reason for my mother's disappearance. I hoped that time would be soon.

I drove straight to Pat's as soon as I arrived in Raven Rock, concerned that my new pet had probably forgotten who she belonged to, from so much handling about. But Cotton only protested meekly when I imprisoned her in her cardboard traveling box. Apparently she was resigned to her fate. Mary Faye looked on grudgingly, naming on her fingers a list of reasons why Cotton should stay with her. Her mother, I noticed, did not encourage her.

Honeysuckle House baked in the late afternoon sun. I dropped my suitcase by the daybed and let the kitten out of her flimsy jail. I would have to get her a scratching post so she wouldn't claw the new draperies and slipcovers when they came. It was going to be a pretty house; the freshly painted walls would provide a soft background for the furniture that would soon arrive. I had selected more from Emmett's attic than I had intended, and I moved from room to room trying to decide just where I would put everything.

I found it in the kitchen. It was propped against the sugar bowl on the enamel table—the group picture of my mother's I had lost at Morgan's cabin. My first thought was that Morgan had returned it, until I saw the red circle of ink drawn around my mother's face and the paper with the message beside it:

I know who you are!
The Chuckler

The note was complete with the childish picture of a clown's face.

My first impulse was to run—back to Shannon, to Emmett, anywhere. After the first wave of fear and nausea passed, anger took over. Was this someone's idea of a joke? Morgan's? Morgan had access to the picture; he also knew I was interested in the Chuckler murders. But did he know of my relationship with Maggie Grey? Obviously someone did. And how did they get in? I tried the back door. It was unlocked! Had I forgotten to lock it? Possibly. I had been in a hurry to leave, and there was nothing valuable in the cottage, nothing anyone would want to steal.

The thought of being alone in that house weighed me down with fear. I felt heavy-limbed, slow-witted. My brain refused to function. The Chuckler, or whoever had returned the picture, could still be hiding in one of the rooms upstairs, waiting for me!

I threw open the back door, started across the yard to Essie's. Seth would know what to do. Then I remembered—Seth probably had a key to the cottage. Seth, Essie, the roomers, any of them could have delivered the picture while I was away. I was instantly ashamed. Seth was away at a convention. It couldn't have been Seth, unless he had returned earlier. And Essie? I might as well suspect my own grandmother! I stopped midway across the yard and turned back to Honeysuckle House. My wild appearance would only frighten Essie and the others. Besides, if the intruder were lurking upstairs, he (or she) could escape unseen while I was out of the house.

I crept back into the kitchen and tiptoed across the hall and into the living room, the kitten pouncing at my stockinged feet. I turned to Morgan's number in the phone book and eased the receiver off the hook. Each click of the dial seemed magnified a thousand times. He answered yawning. A pity I had to disturb his nap.

"Could you come by the cottage for a minute?" I tried to keep my voice low. "Something's wrong."

"Who is this? Speak up! I can't hear you!"

If the Chuckler were upstairs, he would have to be deaf not to hear him. "Damn it," I said, "it's Henri. I need you, right now. I'm scared, Morgan! Please come over."

He caught the urgency in my voice. "Henri? What's wrong? Are you sick?"

"No, I'm not sick," I hissed. "But I might be worse than that if you don't hurry!"

"Be right there!" He hung up, leaving his words trailing in the air.

Now that I had enlisted Morgan's aid, how was I going to show him the message without revealing my identity? Fortunately there was enough space between the first part of the message ("I know who you are!") and the signature so I could tear off the top part without its being obvious. With a damp paper towel I dabbed at the inked circle on the photograph. It came away with only a trace of a pinkish smear that looked as if it could have been caused by age.

I had just completed these concealing maneuvers when I heard Morgan's Jeep outside. He must have broken some sort of speed record to have arrived so quickly. I didn't care. And if the police were on his trail, so much the better. They were welcome.

Grabbing my evidence, I dashed through the back door, pausing only to scoop up Cotton, who seemed determined to trip me before I could get away. I met Morgan at the front of the house as he was bounding up the steps. "Wait! Don't go in yet. Someone could still be inside." I had to stop him.

I did. He covered the distance between us in two giant steps. "What happened? Are you all right? Did somebody . . ."

I dropped the kitten in a drift of leaves and held out the photograph. "Remember this? I found it on my kitchen table when I came home this afternoon." He glanced at the old snapshot, turned it over in his hands.

"Funny, I never did find out what happened to this. Wonder how it got here." He shrugged. "Somebody must have come across it and knew it was yours. I guess they returned it while you were gone." He shook his head, thrusting the picture under my nose. "And you made me rush over here for this?"

Passively, I presented him with the accompanying scrap of paper. "I found this with it."

Morgan frowned, his fingers plowing through his hair in a familiar gesture. "Somebody's crude idea of a joke, but why? That happened so long ago I had almost forgotten it until . . ."

"Until I mentioned it the other day?"

His firm hand encircled my arm, and I found myself being led to the steps and seated in a fragment of sunlight. "Look," Morgan said, "I don't blame you for being scared, but I don't think this is anything to worry about. It couldn't possibly be the Chuckler. That guy's been in prison for years."

I shivered although it was still warm. "Maybe he's out now."

"No way! After killing three people?"

"He could be on parole, couldn't he? Or he might have escaped."

He sat down beside me, examining the printed message. "Think about it, Henri. Why would this man be after you? How would he get that picture? No, I think somebody has a warped sense of humor. They probably didn't mean to scare you, but I can understand why it would make you feel uneasy." He swung his locked fingers between lanky knees and looked at me from the corners of his eyes. "Who else knew you were interested in those murders?"

"Well, Charlie, for one. He helped me find the back issues. And Joyce and Dan, I guess. They were the ones who told me about it." I looked over my shoulder at the massive front door. "I'm afraid to go back inside. How do I know he isn't still there?"

For an answer he sprang to his feet, swinging open the door in one smooth motion. "Are you in there, Chuckler? Ready or not, here I come!"

I jumped up, treading on his shadow. "You're not leaving me out here alone!"

He grinned. "I thought you were afraid to go inside."

"Not if you go first."

We went through the cottage twice, poking into closets, behind stairs, even in the kitchen cabinets. No one was lurking there. In the bathroom, the underwear I had washed on Thursday waved at us from the towel rack. "Hmm," Morgan said, "34B, or thereabout." I pretended not to hear him.

We ended up in the kitchen, the picture and the note still before us. "I think you can rule out Charlie," Morgan said. "And I can't see Joyce or Dan pulling a trick like this. They just wouldn't!"

"I'm not accusing them!" My voice sounded ugly, harsh. It shocked me. "I'm not accusing anyone, but somebody had to do it. I didn't put it there myself!"

He looked at me for a long time. "Nobody said you did, Henri. It just doesn't make any sense. It's only an old photograph. You said it belonged to your mother?"

I nodded. "It was a picture of a friend of hers, a girl who used to live here, that's all."

"Nothing important?" he persisted.

"No. I only brought it to . . . Well, I thought it would be nice if I could find her. Mom died last spring; she said they had been close friends. I think they grew up together. I thought maybe she'd want to know."

He nodded. "I'm sorry. Which one was she, your mother's friend?"

I pointed to Maggie Grey. "It's not a very good picture. You probably can't tell . . ."

110

"Why, that's Maggie, isn't it? Joyce's roommate! Remember? We were talking about her the other night. She left here years ago."

"Oh. Mom always called her Margaret. I . . . I couldn't remember her last name." I moved to the stove, filled the kettle. I needed to do something with my hands. "I think I need a cup of tea. Want some?"

His eyes narrowed. "I think you need something stronger than tea, Henri. Your hands are shaking."

"I don't have anything stronger than beer."

He leaned across the table, snapped off the heat under the kettle. "Well, I do! Come on."

"Where? Where are we going?"

Morgan laughed. "My place, of course! Oh, don't worry, it's perfectly respectable. Dad and Alice are there. In fact, we'll even provide you with supper, not a very elegant one, I'm afraid. We always have sandwiches on Sunday night."

The Lawrence home was only a few blocks away, which accounted for Morgan's seemingly miraculous arrival that afternoon. A woman was raking leaves in the front yard. She shaded her eyes with her hand, then waved as we pulled in the driveway. Morgan returned her greeting with a short blast of his horn. I had been driving most of the day in the same rumpled clothes, and Morgan hadn't allowed me time to comb my hair. "I feel like somebody the cat dragged in," I told him. "We should have called first."

"Why? Alice won't care. She's used to me."

"Is Alice your sister?"

He pulled the Jeep into an attached carport at the side of the porch and reached across me to open the door. "Alice is my mother. She's really my stepmother, but I don't like that word. She and Dad married when

111

I was ten. My own mother died when I was a baby, so she's the only mother I know."

Alice came across the lawn to meet us. A slender, graying woman with a pleasant face, she flicked the leaves from her sweater. "Chip's in the den watching the ballgame." She smiled at me. "But I'll bet we can talk him into joining us for a drink."

"He's not on call then?" Morgan asked.

"Not tonight," Alice explained. "The poor man's probably fallen asleep. He was in late last night, you know."

"Chip?" I smiled at Morgan as he ushered me into the house.

"Dad's nickname," he explained with a wry face. "You know, 'Chip off the old block'!"

Dr. Lawrence was not asleep, nor was he the ancient, white-haired sage Hannah's news story had led me to believe. A wiry, graceful man, he leaned forward in his chair, intent on the game. His dark hair was only spattered with gray above bristling brows.

"You're just the fellow we need to see," Morgan told his father after making the introductions. "Henri has had something of a scare."

"And how was that?" His father made a place for me on the sofa, tossing newspapers to the floor. Alice brought ice from the kitchen, and we sipped our drinks in the warm, paneled den, nibbling on cheese and crackers as Morgan told his family about my experience.

No one said anything for a while after he finished talking. It was such a prepostrous tale, I think they were waiting for a punch line. Alice was the first to take us seriously. "You found these things on your kitchen table?"

I nodded.

"Was there a forced entry?" her husband asked.

I glanced at Morgan, ashamed to admit I had found my door unlocked.

He sliced a thick slab of yellow cheese and sandwiched it between two crackers. "The kitchen door was unlocked," he explained, "but Henri *thinks* she locked it before she left for the weekend."

"These people in the picture," Dr. Lawrence began, "just who were they, and why would anyone be interested in that particular photograph?"

"That's what we'd like to know," Morgan answered. "*Why?* There were several women in the snapshot. One of them was Maggie Grey. Remember Maggie, Dad? I didn't recognize any of the others."

The doctor's eyes drilled into mine. "You knew Maggie Grey?"

"Well, not really," I explained, turning from his probing stare. "My mother did, a long time ago. They went to school together." I rattled the ice in my glass to cover the tremor in my voice. "Morgan says she doesn't live here anymore. Do you know where she went?"

Dr. Lawrence shook his head. "No, we never heard from Maggie after she left here." He looked at the glass in his hand as if it could help him find the words he was searching for. "I realize this is going to put me in a suspicious light," he said, "but I took that picture from your Jeep, Morgan."

His son's face reflected a mixture of irritation and amusement. "Oh, come on, Dad!"

"No, I mean it." Dr. Lawrence put his glass on the table. "I was looking for a map. Remember when your mother and I made that trip to the beach in August?"

Alice threw up her hands. "Rained every day!"

"Anyway," Morgan's father continued, "that's when I saw the photograph. I really didn't look at it well, but I could see it was made at Essie's. I thought it belonged to her, that she had left it in the Jeep." He turned to me. "Since I was going by there later to see Miss Cora, I stuck it in my shirt pocket."

Alice frowned. "What's wrong with Miss Cora now?"

Her husband winked at me. "She has the double Os."

"What's *that*?" I asked, obligingly playing the straight man.

The doctor grinned. "Old and Ornery."

Morgan, stooping to add ice to his glass, gave me a green-eyed glance. "You asked for that one, Henri. But go on, Dad, about the picture. Did you lose it?"

When his father looked up I saw where Morgan had inherited the color of his eyes, but the doctor's eyes were deeper, darker than his son's. They flared now at his question. "I didn't say I lost it, did I? I gave it to Miss Carrie."

"Miss Carrie! Why Miss Carrie?" Alice asked. "Why not Essie?"

"Essie wasn't there, that's why. In fact, I had almost forgotten the blamed thing, but I remembered it as I was leaving. Carrie happened to be the last person I saw. She said she'd see that Essie got it."

Morgan stood at the window staring at the smoky autumn twilight. "Dad, you should have known better than to depend on Miss Carrie for anything. Everybody knows she's as nutty as a fruitcake."

His father's voice was even. "That depends on your definition of 'nutty,' son. We all fit into that fruitcake at one time or another."

I finished my drink and declined Morgan's offer of another. "You don't suppose Miss Carrie . . ."

Dr. Lawrence grunted, shook his head, but his wife disagreed. "She's the most likely candidate so far. You'll have to admit, Chip, she is a bit addled."

"But Carrie's not mean," her husband argued. "Whoever did this is spiteful."

"Or cruel, like the Chuckler," I said. I said it so softly I didn't think anyone had heard me.

I was wrong. "That's impossible," Morgan's father said. "That man couldn't have done it! Why, he's in prison. He may even be dead by now."

"There's one way to find out," Morgan decided. "Call the prison. Ask."

Alice paused on her way to the kitchen. "Which prison? Do you know where he is? I don't."

Morgan stood behind the sofa, his hands resting on the back. I felt the nearness of his fingers against my neck. It was a caring gesture, a possessive one, and it surprised me. It also surprised me that I liked it.

"We can find out where they sent him from back copies," Morgan said. "What do you say, Henri? Would it make you feel better to know he's safely locked away? We can go down to the office after we eat and check this out."

If he had asked me to go to the Black Hole of Calcutta, I probably would have followed him that night. Maybe it was because he had been dependable and kind, had been there when I had needed him. Or maybe it was something more.

Eighteen

I leaned against the counter in the boxlike storage room as Morgan flipped through old editions on the Chuckler trial. The Register office was quiet and dark, and we were the only ones there. I stood at Morgan's elbow watching his profile in the dim light. It was a clean face: straight nose, wide mouth, strong chin. I concentrated on the area between the nose and the chin. "You always seem to be bailing me out of a sticky situation," I said, half-laughing. My hand rested lightly on his arm.

His eyes never left the page. "Looks like somebody has to."

I moved away, leaving room between us, actually only a few inches, but you could have put a continent there. It had been a baiting sentence, one calculated to trigger an emotional response.

Well, he had responded. I had been rebuffed, shrugged off like an indifferent suggestion. I had always considered myself above that kind of thing. It annoyed me to admit to myself that I was every bit as sly as the more feline of my sex. Evidently I had misread his actions at the Lawrence home.

"Here it is, Henri!" He was oblivious to my disappointment. "He was sent to the state prison, and I'll be willing to bet he's still there. Do you want to call or shall I?"

I shrugged. "You do it." I lounged in the doorway of his office while he placed the call; the hard, sharp wood of the door frame cut into my shoulders.

"You certainly seem unconcerned for someone near panic only a few hours ago," he said as we waited for the call to come through.

"Bravado," I said. I hoped he would accept it.

Morgan held his hand over the mouthpiece. "They have to check," he whispered. "It'll take a while. Sunday, you know."

I knew. It had been Sunday forever. I had left the city at midmorning, after stopping to say good-bye to Emmett; I had arrived in Raven Rock much later to find a threatening note; my romantic advances had been coldly rejected. And now I was about to hear a murderer had been released, a murderer who for some implausible reason had decided to make my life a nightmare.

Morgan held up his hand, frowned in an attitude of listening. "Oh? When was that?" he asked. "Are you sure? Yes, yes, of course. Thank you."

"Well?" I watched him slowly replace the receiver, tried to read his expression.

"The man we call the Chuckler is dead," Morgan said. "He died of cancer seven years ago."

I looked at him across the small, cluttered room. I didn't know whether to be sad or happy, to cry or to laugh. "I'm ready to go home," I said. "I imagine the kitten will be hungry." I guess it was a strange thing to say, but just then Cotton was the only warm spot in my life in Raven Rock.

117

"I'll check the house once more, just to be sure," Morgan said as we pulled up outside Honeysuckle House.

"That's really not necessary, but thanks anyway." I hurried to the door. "You've really been nice, Morgan, your family, too, and I do appreciate it." I knew my words sounded like a formal thank-you note, but I didn't know what else to say.

"Runs in the family," he replied, following me inside. "And I *will* check the house, Henri. I want you to get some rest tonight. Otherwise, how will you be able to write that catchy society stuff tomorrow?"

"Suit yourself." I went into the kitchen and opened a can to pacify Cotton's fantastic appetite.

He repeated his rounds, stuck his head in the kitchen door, muttered my name. I looked up; my eyes felt as if I had stayed awake all night.

"Between you and me," he whispered, "I think Miss Carrie's responsible for this. I don't care what Dad says. And I'm almost positive that Essie never laid eyes on that picture." He threw out his arms in a comic pose. "Well, the house is clean, not a beastie in sight! And, Henri, we both know Miss Carrie's harmless, nutty maybe, but harmless. If she is the one responsible, I doubt if she meant to frighten you." He smiled. "Now promise me you'll try to get some sleep."

I tried to smile back, but my lips felt as if they were made of modeling clay. "I will," I said. "And thanks, Morgan."

He looked as if he wanted me to ask him to stay, but I didn't.

Nineteen

All day it had been heavy on my mind, like a lump of soggy yeast dough, expanding, suffocating, blotting out all other thoughts.

Morgan had been impatient. "I don't suppose it will do any good to tell you not to worry," he said as I wrote a simple news article for the third time. He jammed his hands in his pockets, shook his head as if I were beyond help. "Don't let it dominate your life. If you do, you'll be no good to yourself or anyone else. If you're smart, you'll forget it, Henri."

And that was all he had to say on the subject, or any other subject that day. Morgan had his mind on more important matters: Mr. Smith was coming. Mr. Smith, our illustrious publisher, was to be in Raven Rock the end of the week for one of his rare visits. He would be a guest at the Lawrences' lake cabin; therefore Morgan would be unable to accompany us on Saturday's bike hike. I was a little disappointed that he wouldn't be with us, and a lot more disappointed that he didn't seem to care.

But I knew he was right about my obsession with the Chuckler, and I knew I had to get to the bottom of that business about the snapshot.

"Essie, I have to talk with you," I said after work that day. I had found her in the kitchen as usual, cleaning up after the evening meal. Miss Carrie skittered in and out, bringing one item at a time from the hodgepodge on the dining-room table. Essie took a tray from the cabinet, handed it to her without a word. She switched on the water at the sink, regarding me over her shoulder. "There's coffee in the pot. Sit down and pour yourself a cup."

I grabbed a dish towel. "I don't want to sit. I've been sitting all day." I watched her squirt a stream of liquid soap into the water. "I'll dry," I said. "I'm glad Miss Carrie's here. This concerns her, too."

Miss Carrie crept in with the tray, bare except for a bread basket and a few crumpled paper napkins. Essie stopped her before she could return for more. "Wait a minute, Carrie. Henri has something to say to us." She leaned on the sink, a huge wet spot spreading across her stomach. "Now, what is it, Henri? What's wrong?"

I told them about finding the picture and the note from the Chuckler on my return to Honeysuckle House the night before. Essie took a deep breath, started to speak, but I held up my hand. "The Chuckler is dead. Morgan checked with the prison, so it couldn't have been him." I looked at Miss Carrie. "Somebody was playing a joke on me, I guess. Only it wasn't funny, and I'm not laughing."

Essie slapped at the counter with a wet dish cloth. "You say you lost this picture and Morgan found it?"

"Yes, but what we didn't know was, his father saw it and thought it was yours. He said he gave it to Miss Carrie to give to you."

Miss Carrie stared at me blankly. "He *did* give you the picture, didn't he, Miss Carrie?" I asked.

"Picture? Why, I don't know . . ."

"Try to remember, Carrie." Essie folded her arms, soapsuds still clung to her wrists. "Just who was in this picture, and why would Chip think it was mine?"

I was trying to explain when the dining-room door swung open and Seth came in. "Henri! I didn't know you were here. Any more coffee in that pot?" He glanced at the three of us. "What's the matter? Am I interrupting a private conversation?"

"As a matter of fact, I'm glad you're here," his mother said, repeating the details of the incident the day before. "I never received that snapshot, Henri, never saw it. I would remember it if I had." Her brown eyes measured me. "You never told me your mother was a friend of Maggie's. I was fond of Maggie. I'm sure I would have recognized her if I had seen the picture." She sighed. "Carrie, are you *sure* you didn't put it down somewhere? Think now!"

Miss Carrie smiled. "Well, let's see now . . ." She examined the backs of her hands, twisted the ring on her finger. "I believe I do remember something. Perhaps I . . ."

Essie bit back a comment, turned sharply to her son. "Did you see it, Seth? On the hall table, maybe? Or lying about the living room? Anyone might have picked it up, one of the roomers, deliverymen, anyone."

Seth stood at the kitchen window, his hands knotted into fists. He didn't answer his mother right away. "No, no I didn't see it, Mother," he said finally. "Why would anyone want to frighten Henrietta? What point is there

121

in it?" He flicked the dish towel from my fingers, pressed me into a chair. "It's absurd. I don't like it!"

"The whole thing seems childish," I said, "like something a twelve-year-old might do. And I know I shouldn't let it bother me." I suppressed a shiver. "But there's something about it that frightens me. Maybe it's the complete lack of reasoning behind it."

"Here, now." Essie pulled up a chair beside mine, plunked down with a sigh. "You just gather up some things and stay with us for a while. There's a folding cot out in the laundry room. We can put you in there." She made an attempt to laugh. "I never iron anymore, anyway!"

"I can't, Essie. We just got through painting Honeysuckle House, and my furniture is due soon. I refuse to be scared away from my own home. I'm not leaving!"

"Of course not, dear." Miss Carrie's voice was soothing. "And I do wish I could remember about that picture. It seems . . ." She patted my arm absently, her voice trailing off.

I stood abruptly, feeling tears not far away. Kindness affected me that way sometimes. "I have to go now, catch up on the work I didn't do today. I hope you'll understand. I *had* to ask you, in case you had seen the picture, but somehow I knew you hadn't."

"Henri, I wish you'd stay." Essie put a hand on my arm.

"I have a phone," I reminded her. "And you're always in yelling distance." I smiled. "If I do get scared again, believe me, you'll know it!"

Seth stepped outside with me. "I'll walk over with you. It gets dark so early now."

I was glad of his company. We waded across the lawn through the dry October leaves; their rustling filled the silence, overcame the need for speaking. Seth drew my attention to the windows of Honeysuckle House as we stepped out of the trees. They were brilliant with light. "Henri, you should keep your shades down," he said, frowning. "Anyone can see inside, and with you there alone . . ."

"I know." I stared through the windows at my empty living room, illuminated for all the world to see. "I left before it was dark. I really didn't think."

He draped a comforting arm across my shoulders, and I cried like I knew I would. It was almost a relief.

Seth didn't scoff, didn't laugh at me. He only stood there in the darkness and held me close, my hair brushing his chin. When I had finished he lifted my face with one finger, kissed me lightly on the forehead. "Feel better?"

I laughed. "I think I've cried all my frustrations away."

"Good." We walked together to the steps. "Henri, I think this thing is exactly what you said it was, a child's prank. There's a kid who lives just down the street, must be twelve or thirteen. Anyway, he cuts the grass when I'm not around. He could easily have taken that picture, found out somehow or other that it belonged to you. I wouldn't be a bit surprised if he weren't your weekend visitor."

I sniffed. "You're just saying that to make me feel better!"

"It's the only explanation that makes sense. It's hard to be objective about people you're close to, I'll admit, but I really don't think Miss Carrie had anything to do with this. I know, I know. Her mind's slipping. It's funny, she can remember things that happened fifty years ago, but she probably couldn't tell you what she ate for supper tonight! But . . . Oh, hell, Henri, she's a sweet old lady!"

"Yes, she is." I unlocked my door, stepped inside. "A little like the two sisters in *Arsenic and Old Lace*. Remember them?"

Seth didn't smile. "I hope you're not serious." He stepped back. "Now the other roomers, I don't know. Old Amos could be capable, but I doubt it. I'll Sherlock around some, see what I can find out. In the meantime, keep your doors locked. And remember, I'm only a few steps away."

I dutifully pulled down my shades, locked my door, smiling at Seth's fatherly advice. But had it really been fatherly advice? I hadn't missed the expression in his eyes when he kissed me: concerned, yes; fatherly, no! If Seth were in his late thirties as I had guessed, it was possible for him to have been my father, but highly unlikely. I had once asked Joyce why Seth had never married. I could easily see him in the father role, bathing a tubful of toddlers, proudly pushing a baby carriage. He was a good-looking, likable man. It seemed like such a waste, I said.

Joyce had laughed. "He never had to marry, I guess. Not that the girls haven't tried. He probably has a honey in every town between here and Richmond." She had put her head on one side, looked at me through narrowed eyes. "You're not interested, are you? Because if you are, I'm warning you, Henri, you're up against a professional bachelor."

I set up my typewriter on the kitchen table, poured a Coke over ice. I was not about to worry over Seth Honeycutt's love life, or even my own, not with four weddings to write up and a feature story due the next day!

Twenty

We were ready for inspection. The shocking disarray of *The Register* office had oppressed me until I could stand it no longer, and the day before our publisher was to arrive, Pat and I sprang into action. Clouds of dust surged as we dashed wildly about like figures in a film run too fast: polishing; mopping; discarding ancient papers, useless leaflets; stacking books in orderly rows. Even Mildred postponed her long, chummy telephone conversations to shine the grimy windows inside and out.

But at Morgan's office we stopped. He looked up from his typewriter, flashed a challenging glance at the three of us. "Take one step inside this door, and you're fired." He went on typing in his slow, agonizing way, and we left him to wallow in his sty.

"He won't even notice, you know," he said to our departing backs. "In another week it will be dirty again, just like it's always been. Mr. Smith is used to the office the way it is. He doesn't care about things like that." He laughed silently, crouching over his typewriter. "You're doing all that work for nothing!"

He was wrong.

"Well, what's this? What have you done here, Morgan? Looks different!" Clayton Smith was a tall, soft-spoken man who moved with unhurried ease.

"Ah, er, just a little straightening up." Morgan was having a difficult time trying not to look at Pat, Mildred, or me.

Mr. Smith paused to speak with Mildred, exchanged greetings with Pat. I was evidently a surprise. "Well, who's this now?"

I stumbled from my desk as Morgan introduced us, trying to squeeze gracefully from the tight space. It couldn't be done.

"Henrietta, you say?" Mr. Smith drew my name out as if he were learning a new word. He extended a hand. "Glad to have you with us. Are you a native of Raven Rock?" He considered me gravely, his eyes never leaving my face.

I stiffened under his scrutiny and wished he would look somewhere else. "I've only been here a few months, but everyone has been so kind I feel as if I've lived here much longer." I looked at Morgan. He nodded smugly. I had said the right thing.

"And how do you like working at *The Register*? Morgan treating you all right?"

"Oh, I enjoy the work," I said, a malicious smile creeping across my face. "I'd like it even better if he'd let me out of my cage."

The publisher's sandy moustache quivered. "Cage?" He turned to Morgan. "What's this about a cage?"

Morgan propelled him toward the gate. "That's just one of Henrietta's little jokes, sir. She's one of those 'progressive' women, you know." It sounded like a dirty word.

Mr. Smith threw me a quizzical glance over his shoulder. "I see, uh . . . Well, good luck, Henrietta."

126

From the look in Morgan's eyes, I was going to need it. I smiled even wider. "Thank you, Mr. Smith!" I was glad when they went in the editor's office and closed the door. Fortunately it was Friday, and I wouldn't have to see Morgan Lawrence for an entire weekend. Time was on my side.

I thought about Morgan as I dressed for our bike hike the next morning, and for the first time I was glad he had decided not to join us. We met at the school: the McDonalds, Mary Faye, Hannah, three other children, and myself. It was one of those brittle, crystal days, cold and bright, so clear you could almost expect the air to shatter. My hooded sweatshirt felt right at nine in the morning, although I knew I would be pulling it off later in the day. I noticed the others were also dressed warmly, except for Hannah, whose plump legs were mottled beneath her cotton skirt. I led Joyce aside. "Hannah's going to freeze when she starts to ride. Can't we find her some pants?"

Joyce frowned. "It's her dad. I told you how he is. And where would we get them? Mine would be much too large, yours too long, and she couldn't begin to get into Mary Faye's!"

"There must be somewhere we could find a pair," I insisted. "Every kid needs a pair of jeans. It's dangerous for her to go riding like that. Look at that long skirt. It could get caught in the spokes."

Joyce nodded. "You're right." She seemed to be measuring Hannah with her eyes. "You know, I'll bet we could find a pair to fit her in some of our daughter's outgrown things. Seems like I saw some in her closet just the other day, looked like they had hardly been worn. I was going to give them away." She looked from me to Hannah and back again. "I suppose I could run her back to the house in the camper. It would only take a few minutes, but if her old man finds out, it's gonna be your hide, my friend!"

I grinned. "Let's ask her."

Hannah listened solemnly as I explained about the skirt. "My father won't like it," she said, kicking at a pebble. She lifted her face, her eyes glowing. "But *I* would!"

Dan unearthed a ball and bat from the back of the camper to keep the others entertained while Joyce and Hannah were gone. By the time they had returned, I had walked two batters. I felt as if I'd been reprieved when the weathered blue truck pulled into the school yard with a triumphant blast of the horn.

And so we were off: Hannah in her stiff new jeans; me with diminished esteem on the athletic field. We had agreed to bike to Raven Rock Lake where we would eat our picnic lunch and perhaps do some hiking.

It was a festive kind of day. The sun was warm on our backs, showy leaves swirled lazily around us, and now and then small splotches of chalky clouds drifted across the blue, blue sky.

Joyce and I slowed when we reached the lake road and let the others ride ahead. It was not yet noon, and we gladly took advantage of the extra time to relax and enjoy the autumn foliage, the deep peace of the woods. The two of us pedaled along together, silent except for the swish of leaves under our wheels.

Joyce jerked the woolly cap from her head and tossed it in the basket behind her. "You're a quiet one today. Not worried about Hannah's father, are you?"

I had succeeded in shoving the Chuckler's menacing message to the back of my mind, but it was always there, waiting to dominate my thoughts at the least opportunity. It did so now on this restful ride to the lake. It was the first chance I'd had to tell Joyce about my phantom visitor. She was strangely quiet as I talked, nodding now and then, frowning as she guided her bike around ruts in the road.

"Who do you think it was?" she asked at last.

"Morgan thinks Miss Carrie did it, but Seth says it's probably the boy who cuts the grass."

"Bobby Wilson?" Joyce bounced as she hit a bump in the road. "Oh, I don't believe it! I taught that kid for two years. Besides, how would he have known that picture belonged to you? Who was in it? Anybody I know?"

I was reluctant to tell Joyce about Maggie Grey. The coincidence of my "mother's friend" being her roommate was almost too much to accept, but I knew she would find out from someone else if not from me.

Joyce coasted to a stop at the bottom of a hill and waited for me to catch up. "Where did your mother know Maggie?"

"They went to school together," I explained, "years and years ago."

"But why would she think Maggie was here? She left Raven Rock right after Dan and I married."

"Mom didn't know that," I said. "Her friend was living here the last time she wrote."

Joyce concentrated on her front tire as it circled beneath her. "That's strange. Don't you think it's strange, Henri? I don't like it." Her stubby hair stuck out in absurd-looking spikes above troubled blue eyes. "I don't mean to scare you, but there's something wrong here. I feel it. Maybe it has something to do with Honeysuckle House. Maybe you should move out of that place, Henri."

I came very close then to telling her who I was. I needed to confide in someone, tell them the whole truth, but something held me back. How did I know

129

that Joyce hadn't left the note? Or Dan? Someone had already guessed my identity, possibly someone I knew well. Many of these people had known my mother, had observed that I looked something like her. Now I was claiming the evasive Maggie Grey to be a long-lost family friend. But if someone *had* put two and two together, why announce it in such a bizarre way? Why not just come right out and ask, "Henrietta, are you Maggie Grey's daughter?" I would have admitted it gladly, and what a relief it might have been. But no one asked.

I heard the spill of the waterfall, felt the turbulent stirring in my stomach as we rode around the last curve where the lake began. Someone had started a fire, and the smell of woodsmoke mingled with the musty scent of dry leaves. Ordinarily that combination is like perfume to me, but not this time. To me it seemed as if a malevolent miasma oozed from this end of the lake, creeping through the underbrush.

Dan was heating a pot of water for instant hot chocolate. The children were laughing, chasing one another at the water's edge. It was a happy picnic scene, a time for songs and stories, and just being together. Why did I want to run away? I put my lunch with the others on the picnic table and rested my head on my arms.

"Hey, you're not sick, are you?" Joyce slid onto the bench beside me. "I didn't want to frighten you by what I said back there, but I can't just brush it off either." She folded and unfolded the top of her lunch sack.

"But the Chuckler is dead," I said. "Surely there couldn't be another like him in Raven Rock!"

Joyce crumpled a dead leaf in her hand. Her words exploded like a bombshell. "Did you ever consider the possibility that they may have convicted the wrong man?"

Twenty-one

"Hannah won't play chase with me!" Mary Faye complained as we rested after our lunch. "She's afraid she'll get her jeans dirty!"

Joyce smiled. "It's all right, honey. That's what jeans are for."

Hannah stroked a bright denim knee. "But they're almost *new*."

"I'll wash them for you, Hannah," I promised. "They'll look even better then. They're supposed to fade, you know."

She frowned. "I know. I just want to wait a while."

"I'd rather you wear dresses if you're going to act like this," Mary Faye said, pouting. "You're not any fun in jeans!"

Dan jumped to his feet, clapping his hands together. "How about a scavenger hunt? A nature scavenger hunt! Everybody gets a list, and we'll see who can find the most. You'll help us, won't you, Henri?"

I felt more relaxed after eating my lunch, drinking the warm, sweet chocolate garnished with ashes from the fire, but the place still depressed me. I was glad of an excuse to escape from the threatening, black rock, the steady rush of the falls.

"I'll be your partner," Hannah said, taking my hand. She cast a chilling look at Mary Faye. "You'll never find as many as we will!"

"Who needs you?" her friend said, claiming one of the boys as her teammate. I felt trapped in the middle of a scrap between friends and looked to Joyce for help. She shrugged. "They'll be over it in an hour, wait and see."

Hannah and I followed a narrow footpath away from the falls until our trail disappeared, gradually leaving us in a gully of rock and scrub pine.

"Slate rock!" Hannah dashed to scoop up a thin slab. "Now I know we're going to win! What else do we need?"

"Good, Hannah! You found a hard one, but try not to talk so loud or they'll hear us." I looked around, listening for the rustle of footsteps, the giggle of our competitors, but heard nothing. I checked our list. "We have the twig of cedar, the sweetgum ball . . ." I fumbled in my pocket "and the hickory nut. Let's see, now we need a yellow poplar leaf and a persimmon." I started to climb the rocks to the hilly, wooded area beyond. "Let's look up here."

Hannah scrambled up before me, crouching at the top. "We'll never find a persimmon! I don't even know what one looks like."

"Well, I do." I dusted off my pants. "They're like orange plums, only bitter."

The pines grew closer together here, and their brown needles were soft under our feet. We had come a long way from the others, and the feeling of isolation became more apparent as we wandered through the woods. I rested at the base of an oak as Hannah chased off to check out a tree with dwindling, golden leaves. I leaned against the rough bark and closed my eyes. An acorn fell somewhere not too far away. Hannah shuffled through the dry leaves, comparing the foliage.

The sharp snap of a twig brought me to my feet. I glanced at the tangled screen of undergrowth behind me. A branch swayed; a vine fluttered. I could see no one, yet I knew that someone was, or had been, standing there, watching me.

I found Hannah investigating a handful of yellow leaves. She dealt them out slowly. "I don't know which . . ."

"This one," I said, snatching a tulip-shaped leaf. I deposited it with our other treasures and yanked her by the arm. "Come on! Our time's running out. Maybe we'll see a persimmon on our way back."

"Okay, okay," she grumbled. "You didn't have to jerk me!"

We twisted through the trees, our footsteps silent on the pine-padded carpet. Hannah, who had been walking ahead, fell into step beside me. The presence of the unseen watcher was still with us. Each far-off whisper of a leaf, even the stillness of the woods, became an ever-increasing threat. I began to run.

Hannah sensed my panic. "What's wrong?" she panted, trying to keep up with me.

I paused, tried to unlock my face. "We won't win if we don't get back in time, Hannah. We have to hurry!"

She allowed herself to be pulled along. "I don't like this place. It's dark. You don't like it either, do you, Henri?"

We were on the edge of the woods now. Ahead was a field of broom sage studded with small cedars. It was not the way we had come, but at least we would be in the open. I waded into the dry yellow grass. Briars snatched at my pants.

"Green things! Green things are all over me!" Hannah cried, plucking at her jeans.

I looked back at her, painstakingly picking off the beggar's-lice. That was when I saw him, or the lower part of him. A man was standing in the thicket behind us, partially concealed by the trees. Foxlike, he slipped behind some bushes, but I had already seen his khaki-covered legs. And I knew it had not been my imagination that led me to believe we were being watched.

"Let's go!" I tugged at Hannah's sleeve. "It's only a sticky weed. It comes right off. It won't hurt you." Together we trudged, panting, up the hill on the other side and emerged on familiar ground. I sagged against a pine and took long, ragged breaths, relaxing at the sight of the enormous stone chimney, the battered green Jeep parked behind the house, accompanied by a sleek, late-model car.

"I'd sure feel a lot better if I could find a bathroom," Hannah said, wiping an arm across her damp, red face.

I grinned. "You're in luck. This is Dr. Lawrence's cabin, and his son is around here somewhere. I'm sure he won't mind if you use the bathroom." We knocked at the door, no answer. It wasn't locked, so I opened it a crack and called. Still no answer. Hannah was biting her lip. "Oh, come on," I said. "I'll show you where it is."

While Hannah was in the bathroom, I wandered into the kitchen, calling again so we wouldn't be mistaken for intruders. Both cars were outside; the two men couldn't have gone far. I glanced out the window to see if they were on the other side of the cabin, but the yard was deserted. At least the man in the khaki

135

pants had not followed us to the cabin. "I wonder where they could be?" I said aloud to myself.

"Who?" Hannah had come out of the bathroom, still picking off the beggar's-lice.

"Mr. Lawrence and his guest," I said, "and for goodness' sakes, do that outside!"

"They're probably fishing." Hannah sat on the porch steps smoothing the cuffs on her jeans. She squinted into the sun. "Here comes somebody now."

My first impulse was to grab Hannah and dash for the cabin door, until I recognized the man in the khaki pants. Mr. Smith raised his hand in a greeting, and I left Hannah on the steps and went to meet him. "I hope you won't mind," I said, "we took advantage of your facilities." I explained about our outing with the children and the competition of the scavenger hunt.

He smiled, pulling a pipe from his pocket. "I'm sure Morgan would be delighted to share his accommodations. He tells me he often enjoys these excursions too. I'm afraid my being here kept him from joining you on this one."

"Where is Morgan?" I asked.

Mr. Smith packed his pipe with pungent tobacco, carefully, as if it were an art. "He's back at the pier. We've been fishing since noon." He laughed. "So far, no luck!"

I noticed he had come from the direction of the lake, but he carried no fishing gear. "You didn't come through the woods over there?" I pointed across the patch of broom sage. "I thought I heard someone behind us as we were trying to find our way out."

He shook his head. "Afraid not. Probably a squirrel or a rabbit." The tobacco glowed red as Mr. Smith puffed slowly on his pipe. He pointed with it in Hannah's direction. "Who's your little friend?"

136

I told him about Hannah and her new jeans, the problem with her father.

"I hope you haven't bitten off more than you can chew," he said, chomping on his pipe stem. "She does have parents, you know. I wouldn't get too attached."

"Guilty," I admitted. "I can't help but feel sorry for her with a hard father like that. I was adopted. But my parents gave me all the love they had in them, and that was a lot."

"Then you should count your blessings, Henrietta," he said. "Happy memories are something you'll never lose."

"I like this cabin, Henri!" Hannah had rid herself of the last green seed pod. "Do you think Dr. Lawrence would mind if we came back again sometime?"

I smiled. "I think he'd like that, Hannah, but we'd better hurry now. The others will be wondering where we are."

I said good-bye to my employer, and Hannah gravely shook his hand. But as I raced toward the lake after my energetic little partner, I could sense him standing there, watching us until we disappeared from view.

The others had been waiting for us for some time, and I read the relief on Joyce's face as we came into the clearing. "Where have you been?" she exclaimed. "I was really beginning to worry."

I told her about the man in the woods and our stop at Morgan's cabin. "Did any of the others look over in that area?" I asked, noticing that Dan also wore khaki trousers.

Joyce shook her head. "No, we walked all the way around the lake." She staggered, as if her knees were giving way. "I must be crazy! I'm getting too old for this. I thought surely you'd be back here waiting for us."

I noticed that Mary Faye and her partner were triumphantly proclaiming their victory, joyfully displaying battered treasures, including a mashed persimmon. But Hannah didn't seem to mind, and soon the two of them were off on their own, arm in arm, whispering secrets that only ten-year-olds can relish.

We started back soon after that, for a cool wind had come up, and the few puffy, white clouds of the morning had gathered and turned to gray.

Hannah changed back into her skirt at Honeysuckle House before meeting her mother at the school, and I felt a little guilty as I tossed her jeans into the basket with my other soiled clothes. I would wash them and keep them for her until our next outing. It was only a little secret, but it was deception just the same. I was helping the child disobey her parents, no matter how I rationalized. Maybe Mr. Smith was right. Maybe I had bitten off more than I could chew. But somehow I didn't care.

I was tired that night, but it was a good tired. It was a treat to climb into my very own bed instead of sleeping on the daybed downstairs. My belongings had arrived earlier that week, and Seth had helped me to place the furniture where it belonged, lifting a heavy chest of drawers with apparently no effort; hoisting my bulky mattress and springs into place with little help from me.

I sat propped in my sturdy maple bed, reading a few chapters from one of my old books, also brought from home. It was like making friends all over again, but I was tired and sleep came early.

The shrill ringing of the phone woke me in the darkness, and it took me a few moments to come to terms with it. I shook off my grogginess, flipped on the hall light, and took the stairs two at a time. Phone calls at two o'clock in the morning usually meant bad news, and my grandmother immediately came to mind. She had been fine when I called her earlier in the week, but she could have taken ill.

"Hello," I said. My hand gripped the back of the wicker chair, felt its woven texture being imprinted on my palm.

It started with a muted rattle, a ragged breath. I stiffened. Not that! Had I rushed downstairs, frightened out of my wits at the whim of some crazy prankster? I was about to hang up when the laughter began, slow, calculated laughter, just above a whisper, the deep-throated trill of chuckles, rasping, evil, hideous!

I don't know how long I stood there listening to that blood-chilling sound. When the fright in me abated, I slammed down the receiver, then took it off the hook and went back upstairs to bed, taking the kitten for company.

I thought of Seth and Essie only a few yards away. If I told them what had happened, I knew they would insist that I move in with them. I wasn't going to give up my beautiful cottage because of some demented caller!

Leaving the hall light on for comfort, I snuggled beneath the covers listening to my own breathing. I dreaded for sleep to come and not to come. Just before I dozed again, I remembered with satisfaction that I hadn't screamed, hadn't said a word.

Twenty-two

"Hannah likes your cabin," I told Morgan the following Monday. "She wants to be invited there again." We were standing around the coffee urn, fortifying ourselves with "instant awakeness" to begin a new week.

He took a testing sip from his cup. "I'm inviting." He was pleased. "She really likes it, huh?"

I laughed. "She told me she'd never seen a log bathroom before!"

"Clayton told me about your visit Saturday. Sorry I missed you." He touched my shoulder. "Why not bring the kids up next weekend? Say, on Saturday. Bring their sleeping bags, make a night of it."

I groaned. "I don't know if I can take two Saturdays in a row! But I'll ask Joyce. If she can take it, I can!"

I leaned against the wall, held the hot mug between my palms. "The Chuckler called last night," I said.

"Henri!" He started to smile, then looked at me closer. "You're serious, aren't you?" His hand tightened on my arm. "Who . . . What did he say?"

"He chuckled, of course, what else?"

Morgan's voice dropped. "Are you joking?"

I met his gaze. "Would I joke about a thing like that? Anything that gets me out of bed at two in the morning is not funny!"

He thumped down his mug. "Did you find out anything from Essie about the picture? What about Miss Carrie?"

I shrugged. "Not much. Miss Carrie doesn't remember the picture, and Essie says she never saw it. Seth thinks the yard boy took it, but this didn't sound like any boy last night!"

"Who did it sound like? Could it have been a woman?" Morgan asked.

"Possibly, if she disguised her voice, but not Miss Carrie! Definitely not Miss Carrie!"

He frowned. "Maybe you should talk to the police, Henri, let them know what's going on."

"But that's just it," I said. "Nothing is, not really. One silly note and a phone call—the police would think I was paranoid."

And maybe I am, I thought later as I sat at my typewriter. I was supposed to be writing a lead for a story on the garden club's autumn tour. Instead I considered the possibility of Essie's roomers masquerading as the Chuckler.

Of the two Waverly sisters, Miss Cora was the more likely candidate. I had witnessed her verbal attacks on her sister, observed her cynical outlook on life. Yet I couldn't see the frail old woman making threatening phone calls at two in the morning or creeping into an empty house to leave that ridiculous note. Nor could I believe that Amos Tomlinson, reluctantly concluding his dreary existence in a lonely room, could be my tormentor. Unless I was a poor judge of human nature, he lacked both the imagination and the energy required to frighten anyone.

That left Howard Lucas, the jovial hardware merchant. I liked Howard. He seemed by far the most conventional of Essie's assorted lot, and my conversations with him had always been pleasant. Yet, as I was constantly being reminded, things or people are not always as they seem.

I had learned from Morgan that all of Essie's roomers had lived in Raven Rock at the time of the Chuckler murders. And, with the exception of Amos Tomlinson, all had been staying at the boardinghouse. They had shared their lives with Maggie Grey, as they were now sharing them with me. And one of them, perhaps, hungered to share something more, something dreadful that I did not want to know about.

I had looked forward that afternoon to a story assignment on the local haunted house that was an annual project of the Raven Rock PTA and was not surprised to find Joyce McDonald in the middle of the grisly decorations. She called to me from the end of a gloomy hallway in the empty house the group was using for their attraction. "Henri! Come and see what we have for Dracula!"

I recoiled when I saw the stark, black coffin, although I had more or less expected it. She laughed. "Borrowed it from the funeral parlor. Lovely thing, isn't it?" She gave it an affectionate pat. "Any bad effects from the bike hike?"

I grinned. "Muscular or otherwise?"

"Either one." She climbed on a chair to drape fake cobwebs from the window.

"Morgan wants to take the kids on an overnight Saturday," I said.

She disentangled a clinging strand from her hair. "Where?"

"His cabin at the lake. Hannah fell in love with it."

She laughed. "Hannah falls in love with everything! Well, Dan and I weren't planning anything for this weekend. I don't see why we shouldn't if the kids want to go." She sighed. "I guess we'd better go on and plan on it. Next week is Halloween, and it gets too cold in November. You'll come with us, won't you?"

"Sure," I said, steadying the chair as she stepped down. "Why not?"

Joyce tilted her head, mocked me with her shrewd eyes. "Why not, indeed?"

Twenty-three

In spite of my casual attitude, I was looking forward to our night at the cabin. When Morgan touched me, as he had done so casually that morning over coffee, for a moment it made my life seem special, set apart. I had to steel myself to remember that our relationship was, at best, indifferent. I was no one special to Morgan Lawrence, and that was fine with me.

I told myself that as we sat around the crackling bonfire. The trees loomed dark, nebulous around us; the icy lake was a black mirror in the distance. But in our circle all was bright, glowing, and slightly cold on the side away from the fire.

"Well, I've learned one thing," Morgan said beside me. "You can't toast marshmallows wearing gloves!" He pulled them off, stabbed another puffy candy with the end of his stick.

"Pass me another one, too," Hannah called, stuffing an oozing, charred marshmallow in her mouth.

"Hannah, you're going to be sick," I warned her. "Don't eat any more. You've already had three hot dogs."

"Don't be a spoilsport! This is a party. Let the kid have fun." Morgan tossed her the bag of candy and was rewarded with a sticky smile.

Dan stood, reluctant to leave the fire. "I guess we'd better get the bedding in from the camper. Come on, kids, give me a hand."

His proposal was met with a chorus of groans as the children clung to the fringes of warmth. Morgan laughed. "Never mind, I'll go. I'll need to start a fire in that fireplace sometime. Might as well do it now and get the cabin warmed up."

Joyce stretched her toes to the fire. "Don't anybody call on me for help. I feel a ghost story coming on." She gazed around her at the inky shadows, her voice taking on a mournful quality. "Did you ever hear about the ghost of the lake?" The children crept together in a huddled group, giggling.

Hannah plucked at my sleeve. "Henri, I don't feel so good. I think I'm . . ."

I resisted the impulse to say, "I told you so," and rushed her to the fringes of the clearing.

"What's the matter with Hannah?" Joyce looked up from her story.

"Too much fun," I explained, starting for the cabin. "We'll need a damp cloth."

"I'll get one!" Mary Faye ran past me. I had started back to where Hannah crouched in the shadows when she suddenly bolted to her feet and ran screaming to the campfire.

"What is it, Hannah? What's wrong?" Joyce and I converged on the shaking child, led her to a seat by the fire.

"It's a man! Out there. I saw him!" She threw her arms around me, buried her face in my shoulder. "He had on a clown's face!"

Joyce's eyes met mine in the firelight. "Oh, Hannah, honey, there's no man out there. You must have seen a shadow."

"No! I tell you, I saw him!"

Mary Faye arrived with the towel and huddled over us as I blotted Hannah's face. "Will she be okay?"

"She'll be fine. If you really want to help, get someone to go with you and see if you can find the men." I tried to speak calmly. "And tell them to hurry!"

"It could have been a joke," Joyce mumbled, partially to herself. "Someone teasing the children."

It seemed like an eternity before we heard running footsteps and Morgan sprinted into the firelight. His face was set. "What's all this? What's this about a man?" Dan followed, herding a noisy band of frightened children.

We explained to them what Hannah had seen, and both men checked the area thoroughly with flashlights. "There's no one here," Morgan called as they returned from their search. "If there was a man, he's gone now."

Hannah sat up straighter, shrugged off her damp towel. "He *was* there."

Dan smiled. "There is a bush over there, Hannah. It looks a little like a clown. You were sick and scared. Don't you think maybe you could have . . ."

"No!"

"Well, just come and look at it. See if you don't think that could be what frightened you."

"No!" Hannah shifted closer to me. "I don't want to."

"You don't have to, Hannah." Joyce gathered the children around her. "But we do have to get inside and get some sleep. It's late."

"She's right," I agreed. "We'll build a big fire in the fireplace, and you can spread your sleeping bags right there on the floor where it's warm."

"Can we whisper?" Mary Faye wanted to know.

"For a while," Dan said, "but only a little while."

"A little while" turned out to be nearly one o'clock in the morning. By the time everyone had brushed his teeth, gone to the bathroom for the third time, and called out the last "good night," I was exhausted.

After everything was quiet, Morgan and I went outside to clean up the debris from the picnic, while the McDonalds prepared for bed in the one small bedroom. Inside, the children were at least pretending to be asleep, but now and then I could hear Joyce or Dan issuing threats from their open door.

The bonfire had burned down to a flicker of a flame as we prepared to douse it for the night. Morgan stared into the winking embers and sank onto a log, patting the place beside him. "Seems a shame to put it out," he said. "Sit down. Let's talk a while."

I sank gratefully beside him. It was the first peaceful moment of the night.

"Do you think Hannah really saw something out there?" Morgan asked, poking the embers into a feeble glow.

"I don't know. She has an imagination, but she wouldn't deliberately lie."

"If she hadn't been sick, she wouldn't have seen her phantom in the clown's face," Morgan persisted.

"Listen, if there *was* a man out there, he wanted us to see him. He would have a found a way!"

Morgan's hand covered mine. "So you think there really was a man out there? Henri, don't be frightened. We'll look again in the morning, see if he left any traces."

147

I drew my hand away, held it to the fire. "What good will that do? You really don't believe she saw anything. I doubt if you believe me either!"

Morgan was silent. I heard him stand beside me, reach for the shovel. "Guess we'd better put out the fire." He sprinkled dirt over the last gasping flames, leaving a mound of warm, orange ashes. I stood there watching, like a mourner at a funeral, as he scooped up a second shovelful. "You can go on in, Henrietta. I know you must be cold."

I jammed my hands deep in my pockets. "I'm not cold."

He turned his back to me and finished burying the fire, propped the shovel against the house. Still I stood by the remains of the bonfire, compelling myself not to shiver.

"Henri?" He touched my arm. I turned to find him standing behind me. "Why do you irritate me so?"

His arms eased around me, held me. His lips brushed my hair. It was the most natural thing in the world. When he kissed me, it was as if we had kissed one thousand times before.

The next morning Hannah squatted over my sleeping bag, a tousled braid trailing across my face. "We heard you and Morgan come in last night."

"Go away," I said.

She giggled. "I'll bet you thought we were asleep, didn't you? You were out there kissing, weren't you?"

"Get your knee off my stomach, and mind your own business." I tried to turn over, dump her off.

She tugged at the zipper on my bag. "Get up, it's time to eat. I'm hungry! What are we having for breakfast?"

148

"Breakfast? I'm surprised you can even talk about food after last night!"

But greedy Hannah had apparently forgotten her illness of the night before. Nor did she mention the frightening visitor she had seen in the ebbing circle of firelight. I expected her to be afraid to go outside, but after our breakfast of oatmeal and cocoa, she ran out to explore with the others and came in later with a wrinkled persimmon. "Look, Henri! I finally found one." She held the fruit on a mittened palm. "There's all kinds of neat stuff around here. I like this place. It's nice here. Do you reckon we'll ever get to do this again?"

"I'm sure of it," I said, "but not if we don't clean it up before we leave."

I was on my way to the camper with an armload of bedding when Mary Faye dodged past in hot pursuit of a giggling boy. "Mrs. McDonald wants you!" she yelled. "Out behind the cabin."

She gained on her quarry and tackled him. He didn't seem to mind.

I found Joyce beside the buried remains of the bonfire, absently poking at the ashes with a charred stick. She looked older in the gray light, her mouth drawn into a grim line.

"There's something I want to show you, over here." She led me to the scraggy area where Hannah had seen the apparition the night before. "Dan found this early this morning. He didn't want me to tell you, but I think you should know." She pointed to a small, bare section of ground where the underbrush had been pulled away. There, etched on the claylike soil, was the malignant likeness of a clown's face.

Twenty-four

"Miss Meredith, will you please come to the principal's office?" The school's ancient intercom sqawked and sputtered. I assigned my class a Halloween story to write and went downstairs to the office, fighting the fear of being so abruptly summoned. The school secretary cast me a sympathetic look as I tapped on the door to the inner office. I crept inside to find Joyce scrunched in the defendant's chair across from Miss Bertie's desk, while a giant man in overalls paced between them.

"I don't like my girl wearing britches," the man sputtered, "and I'd like to know who took it upon themselves to go against my authority!"

Miss Bertie observed the ranting figure with a cold eye, then nodded curtly to me. "Sit down, Miss Meredith." I sat. Joyce stared knowingly at me with an "I told you so" expression. I felt my defenses wither.

"Mr. Whitaker tells me that he believes the two of you gave Hannah a pair of jeans," Miss Bertie began.

"I don't believe. I know!" Hannah's father thundered, pointing an accusing finger at me. "You didn't think I'd find out about it, did you? But I did. Kids talk. It got back to me what you'd done!" The man's face was red with fury. "Your sins will find you out!"

"Mr. Whitaker!" Miss Bertie's voice cut like a knife. Her command was evident. "I won't have my teachers addressed in such a manner! Not by you, not by anyone. Now, if you'd like to discuss this sensibly, please sit down."

He sat, plucking at his faded demin cap with trembling fingers. "It ain't right," he muttered. "I've tried to raise her right, teach her to respect her parents, fear the Lord!" Mr. Whitaker darted a look at me as if I were in league with the devil.

"And you've done a good job, Mr. Whitaker," I said. "Hannah's a good child, one of the nicest ones I know, and talented, too. I hope you won't blame her because of something I did. It was a cold morning, and it's even colder when you're on a bike. We just didn't want Hannah to be sick."

He brooded into his cap. "Humph, don't like her on that bike either. Warn't my idea to let her have one. She's got no business off gallivantin' around like she does! Ought to stay home where she belongs."

"Surely, Mr. Whitaker, you can't deprive the child of her few . . . her moments of play." Miss Bertie leaned over her desk. "She's only a child. She needs to have fun, be with other children. Everyone deserves a little freedom now and then."

He stood abruptly. "Don't tell me about freedom! We had one that had a little too much of that! I don't want Hannah turning out bad like her sister Elsie."

"Hannah is not her sister, and she's not bad," Joyce protested. "And neither is Elsie. She just made a mistake. We all make mistakes, Mr. Whitaker." She added the last sentence softly, but I think he got her meaning.

151

He jammed his cap on his head with such force I was surprised it didn't tear. "Well, I'll tell you one thing, lady, you made one when you gave her them pants!" He jerked open the door. "You can just take them pants and . . . and throw'm in the trash!" The door slammed behind him.

Joyce and I took one look at one another and burst into laughter. Miss Bertie's silence led me to expect the worst. I was awed to find her laughing, too, her glasses awry as she wiped away the tears. "Insufferable man!" she muttered. "Poor little Hannah. I know I shouldn't take this lightly, but he's really more than I can take with a straight face!"

Joyce and I exchanged relieved smiles as we left the office. Not only had our formidable principal supported us in our adversity, I was almost certain she agreed with us.

"Your Mr. Smith was right," I told Morgan later at the office after relating our experience. "I guess I did bite off more than I could chew."

He laughed. "When you stick your nose in a wasp's nest, Henri, you should expect to get stung! But I wouldn't worry about it. Now that Papa Whitaker's had his say, you'll probably never hear from him again."

"I certainly hope not," I said.

It had been a long day, and I had to stop for groceries on the way home. I hurried to the back door of Honeysuckle House with the ingredients for my dinner crammed in a splitting paper sack. I was glad to be at home and looked forward to a leisurely meal alone in my own kitchen. I dumped the bulging bag on the table and scrabbled for a can of cat food at the bottom of the sack. It was liver, Cotton's favorite flavor, and I looked around for the kitten as I spooned the meat in her dish. She was usually twined around my feet as soon as I opened the door.

"Kitty? Here, Kitty!" I looked in her box, thinking she might be asleep, but she wasn't anywhere in the house.

Anxiously, I ran into the yard, calling, searching in all her favorite places. I couldn't understand how Cotton could have gotten outside unless she had zipped through the door as I was leaving for work that morning. Frightened now, I made my way through the leaves to the other side of the cottage. A stab of pain went through me as I glimpsed the limp, white form. "Oh, Cotton! Cotton!" I cried, dreading to touch the small, stiff animal. She lay in a damp mound of leaves, her green eyes glassy in death, a short length of twine twisted around her tiny neck! I picked her up and winced at the scrap of paper that had been beneath her body. I had sensed it would be there. Shaking with rage, I crumpled the note into a wad and stamped it into the ground. It wasn't until later that I thought to be afraid of the Chuckler's intimidating message: "You're next!"

Twenty-five

"You'll have to get out of Honeysuckle House!" Essie leaned across the cluttered kitchen table, grasped my hands in hers. I wondered at the strength in her stubby fingers. "It's wrong for you, Henri. I've felt it from the start." Her eyes implored me. "You're in danger there."

The police had come and gone, taking with them the two notes and the snapshot. "The work of a sadistic loony," the detective said. They listened to my rambling story of the phone call, the incidents at the lake. They asked questions, took notes. I wasn't so sure they didn't think I was the loony, that I had made it all up, except for the cat. Surely they didn't think I had killed my own kitten. Poor Cotton! She would have been better off if we had left her to take her chances in the cotton patch.

I fumbled in my pocket for a tissue. My eyes were red from crying; my head ached. Morgan had been sitting next to me.

"Do the police have any idea who could be doing this?" he asked.

I shook my head. "Not yet. They're working on it."

"Henri!" He gripped my shoulder. "I hate to even suggest this, but remember what you told me this afternoon about your confrontation with Mr. Whitaker? You don't suppose he . . ."

"Oh, no! No, I don't think so. He's strange, but he wouldn't do a cruel thing like that! Besides, this has been going on for weeks, before we even gave Hannah those jeans."

Morgan frowned. "But he's obviously unstable. He probably resents your friendship with Hannah, has been resenting it. He's a fanatic, Henri. People like that have strange reasons for the things they do."

"I don't know, Morgan, maybe he could have," I admitted. "I'll mention it to the police if you think I should, but I don't want to get the man in trouble if he's innocent."

"If he's innocent, he has nothing to worry about," Essie pointed out. "Meanwhile, I want you to find a suitable place to stay, away from here, away from Honeysuckle House." She shoved a graying wisp of hair from her face. "This wickedness . . . it's wrong . . ."

"Oh, Essie!" I reached across to her, hoping for some last surge of inner strength to share with this woman. "Don't you realize that if this person wants to hurt me, he's going to try it no matter where I am? The longer I put off going back to Honeysuckle House, the harder it's going to be."

Her eyes were wide in confusion. "Surely you're not going back to that house tonight, alone?"

"The police have promised to patrol the area," I said. "They'll check on me. And I'll call Pat or Joyce. I'm sure one of them could spare a night or two away from home, just until things calm down."

"Better still, I'll call for you." Morgan shoved his chair away from the table. I heard him dialing in the hall.

"Mary Faye's sick, and Pat can't leave her," he told us, hurrying back into the kitchen, "but Joyce said she'll be glad to come. She'll be here in half an hour." He placed his hands on my shoulders, nuzzled my hair with his chin. "Come on, I'll walk over with you. We'll wait for her together."

I stood numbly in the living room of the cottage while Morgan double-bolted the door. The house smelled strongly of honeysuckle, affecting me like an anesthetic. I sank onto the daybed, strangely sleepy.

Morgan smiled down at me. "That's right. You get some rest. I'll put on some coffee."

"I'll go with you." I followed him into the kitchen, trying to shake off my dull heaviness. He turned from the sink where he was filling the coffee pot. "Look at you! You're afraid to stay alone in your own living room, and you say you want to go on living in this house." He slammed the pot on the stove. "What's wrong with you, Henri? What aren't you telling me? There's something, I know there is, something you're holding back."

"Why do you think that?" My voice sounded false, even to me. I struggled to hold up my head.

"Why you, Henrietta? Why is somebody doing this to you? There must be a reason! You know what it is. Why won't you tell me?"

I rubbed my eyes. "Believe me, I would if I knew."

"It's something about that picture, isn't it? The snapshot made at Essie's. There must be some connection between that old picture and the Chuckler murders."

"Morgan, I honestly don't know," I said. "I gave it to the police. Maybe they'll figure it out. What do you suppose they'll do with it?"

He took mugs from the cabinet, fished in the drawer for spoons. "Blow it up, I guess, you know, make it larger. Even Essie couldn't tell who all those people were. Maybe someone will be able to recognize them."

I nodded. "You recognized Maggie Grey."

"Only because you pointed her out, and because I knew her as a child." He sat back in his chair, his long legs stretching almost across the small kitchen. "The rest of them I don't remember, but maybe if we can get a good look at the people in that photograph it will jog somebody's memory."

I propped my chin in my hands and watched the steam puff from the spout of the coffee pot. Somewhere, someone was seething inside, not unlike the bubbling brew. "I hope so," I said. "Something has to happen soon."

"Is that what you're waiting for, Henri? Something to happen? Is that why you refuse to leave this place?"

There was no way I could escape his prying gaze. "Yes," I admitted finally.

"But you're not going to tell me about it, are you?"

"No, not yet, Morgan. I can't."

He took the pot from the stove, poured hot, black liquid into the waiting mugs, avoiding my eyes. "I'm sure you must have a reason, Henri. I hope it's a good one."

"Morgan," I began, "it's something I can't explain, something even I don't understand yet. Please, be patient just a little longer. Don't give up on me yet."

He pulled me into his arms as though I were a rag doll. "Now whatever makes you think I'd do a stupid thing like that?"

157

I resented the slam of Joyce's car door in the driveway, the sound of her voice at the door. Morgan brushed my face with a last kiss, making an effort to smooth my hair. He smiled. "I'll get the door." I heard him move across the living room, slide back the bolt. The two of them spoke in whispers, then Joyce called out brightly, "Hey, is that coffee I smell? Hope you've saved me a cup!"

I echoed a greeting, turned on the burner under the pot. My hand trembled as I reached for a cup. I had asked Joyce to be my "bodyguard" for the night, but how was I to be certain she wasn't the person I was guarding against?

Twenty-six

The wind whipped sodden leaves into a bleak sky as I drove Joyce to school. A cold rain lashed at the car windows, pummeling the pavement with a force that made driving difficult.

"Sure hope this lets up by tonight." Joyce frowned at the rain-swollen gutters as we crept through the early morning traffic. "The kids can't go trick-or-treating in weather like this."

I eased under the school awning, wipers flapping. "Not unless they swim! But you'll still have your haunted house, won't you?"

She gathered her books together, pulled a hood over her head. "Oh sure, business as usual." She touched my arm in a parting gesture. "Listen, Henri, we'll be through by ten. You know I'll be glad to stay with you tonight, or better still, come home with Dan and me. I don't want you staying over there alone on Halloween."

"Joyce, I'm not asking you to give up another night to babysit with me! You've already been away from Dan for two nights now. I feel like a home-wrecker!"

She laughed. "It's good for him! Makes him appreciate me. Promise me you'll stay at Pat's or Morgan's if not with us. I'm worried about you, Henri."

The cars were lining up behind us. An impatient motorist pounded his horn, and Joyce swooped into the rain, slamming the door behind her. "I'll see you in class!" I called.

I maneuvered the rain-swept streets, ashamed of my earlier suspicions. Joyce had been a stabilizing solace during the past two days. I had relied on her sensible judgment. But it was possible to ask too much, even of a friend. We would be working late at the paper that night, putting together a special anniversary edition of *The Register.* Pat had offered the pull-out sofa in her den, and I planned to take advantage of her invitation. I had no intentions of coming home alone to Honeysuckle House, not on Halloween night!

Mildred glanced at me sharply as I walked in, her usually ruddy face pale. "There's a policeman to see you, Henri. He's back in Morgan's office." Her nose fairly twitched with curiosity.

The officer stood as I entered. It was Lieutenant Griswold, the detective I had spoken with two days before. He nodded. "Miss Meredith, would you sit down, please?"

Morgan hesitated by my chair, touched my face in passing. "I suppose you'll want to talk alone. I'll see that you're not disturbed." He paused at the door. "I'll be in Charlie's office if you need me."

The policeman drew an eight-by-ten, black-and-white glossy from its manila envelope and placed it on the desk. "Now, Miss Meredith, we'll have to know just how you came by this photograph and your connection with the woman in the picture."

160

"I told you," I said. "Margaret Grey was a friend of my mother's. She . . ."

He shook his head, kept shaking it. "I don't want to frighten you, Miss Meredith, but the women in this picture have now been positively identified by Essie Honeycutt. Every one of those people were victims or near-victims of the Chuckler, except for your friend Margaret Grey!" He leaned over me, his voice commanding. "Now, what we want to know is, just who is this Margaret Grey, and where can we find her?"

I reached for the picture, studied it silently. "I don't know where she is. She disappeared years ago. I was hoping to find her here."

He leaned against Morgan's desk, folded his arms. "And you say you're doing this for your mother?"

My eyes met his briefly, admitting what he had probably already guessed. "Maggie Grey *was* my mother," I said.

His eyes narrowed. "Then your father's name was Meredith?"

I shrugged. "I was adopted. I don't know my father's name. I don't even know my own name. Smith, probably, or Jones!" I tried to smile. "I was raised by the Merediths since my mother left me with them as an infant. Until last summer I thought I *was* a Meredith."

He tapped the envelope against the palm of his hand. "And you haven't seen your mother in all this time?"

I shook my head, explaining the circumstances of my adoption, my mother's disappearance.

He nodded, frowning as if I had placed him in an uncomfortable situation. "And you traced her back here, to Raven Rock?" He was still a fairly young man, in his midthirties perhaps, yet his manner attested to years of experience on the force. His shrewd gaze held

161

me now. "Does anyone else have this information about your being the daughter of Margaret Grey?"

"I haven't told anyone," I explained, "but apparently someone guessed." I told him about the first note I had received with the return of the snapshot and the part I had torn away.

He frowned, shaking his head. "But I don't understand. Why would you keep your identity a secret? Surely it would have made your search easier if the facts were known."

"Look, Lieutenant, my mother disappeared twenty-two years ago! No one has seen her since, not even her own mother." I paced the small office. "You'll have to admit it's a strange situation. I can't explain it, pass it off as a feeling." I turned to face him. "But it's a strong feeling, almost a *knowing*. I don't want these people to know who I am, not yet. Please try to understand!" I reached out, almost touched him. "You will, won't you?"

He gathered his papers together, crammed them in a leather case. "I can't see that it'll do any harm. On the other hand, I can't see much good from it either." He fastened the case with a businesslike snap. "I don't suppose you'd know who took that snapshot, would you? The photographer, I mean?"

I stared at him dumbly.

He frowned. "I thought not. Essie Honeycutt doesn't know either. She can't even remember when it was made, but she was able to tell us how these women were connected to her rooming house."

"One of them lived there," I said, "my mother's roommate, Nell—"

"Yes, Nell Gordon lived there," he answered. "So did another of the victims, at least for a while. The widow, Loretta Eddington, the one who was killed in

162

her shop, lived at Essie's for several months before she bought a place of her own. And the Tatum girl was a student of your mother's. Essie said she often came by for help with her sewing projects."

"But there was another woman," I reminded him. "One who got away. Is she the other person in the picture?"

"Ann Taylor." He held the bulging briefcase against him. "Mrs. Honeycutt said that the Taylors took their Sunday meals with them now and then, nothing regular. But then a lot of people did."

"Yet they all had some connection there," I said. My throat felt strangely dry.

"Except for one." Officer Griswold stopped, his hand on the doorknob. "The last girl—the child who identified the Chuckler in court—she wasn't in the photograph."

"Do you think she wasn't meant to be a victim? What was she, an afterthought?" I stood in front of the door, barring his way. "Wait a minute! You have to tell me. Do you think that child was attacked by the same person, or did she identify the wrong man as the Chuckler?"

He shook his head, waiting for me to move aside. "We just don't know, Miss Meredith. Right now it looks like there may have been two different people involved. The one they arrested had been seen running away from the child. There's little doubt that he was *her* attacker. About the others, we don't know."

"Then that would mean that somebody, somebody who knew those women, posed them for a picture . . ." I tried to swallow the lump in my throat. "Then, one by one, he executed them, or tried to!"

He looked tired standing there. "It would seem that way. That's why we'd like to find out who the photographer was." His hand fell on my shoulder. "I think you should leave Honeysuckle House, Miss Meredith. Get as far away from Essie's as you can. We can patrol the area; we can even assign a man to protect you. But we can't guarantee you won't be hurt."

I stood there numbly as he opened the door. "Whoever took this picture years ago could still be here in town. If he killed three women then, he wouldn't think twice about doing the same to you." His voice dropped to a whisper as we walked into the newsroom. "Please, take my advice and go. Don't give him the chance!"

Twenty-seven

Hannah remained in her seat that day as the others left the class. I had been feeling strangely elated, considering the detective's gloomy predictions. The children had published a Halloween edition of their newspaper. We had spent the entire period stapling the pages and delivering copies to classrooms. It was a good feeling, a feeling of satisfaction and accomplishment, and one I didn't often experience. It 'was short-lived.

Hannah approached me shyly, head down, as I cleared the cluttered working area. "I'm sorry about Cotton, Henri, you know I am. But my daddy didn't do it! He was at work." Two large tears jerked down her face.

"Oh, Hannah, I know he didn't! It's just that the police had to check all possibilities. We had to be sure." I didn't know what to do, what to say. I wanted to hug her, but I was afraid she would push me away. I held out my hands. "Hannah, please try to understand. We never thought your father would do that."

She ignored my hands and clasped me firmly about my waist. "He wouldn't, Henri! I know he wouldn't! He's different from other people's dads, I know, but he wouldn't hurt anything."

"I know," I said. "I hope you didn't get into too much trouble over those jeans."

She blew her nose into a crumpled tissue. "I didn't. Well, not much, anyway. He just won't let me wear them anymore, won't let me go on any more outings, either. He doesn't like for me to do anything fun!"

"I'm sorry, Hannah. I wish there were something I could do." I pulled her braids back from her face, straightened her collar. "You look nice, you know, in whatever you wear."

She smiled. "It's nice to have someone on my side!" she said. She gathered up her books. "You'll have to write me a pass. I'm late for lunch!"

Joyce waited outside my door, one eyebrow raised. "What was that all about?"

I closed the door of my room behind me, eager to get back to the newspaper. "The kitten. Hannah says her father was at work. He couldn't have done it."

"Yeah, I know." She studied my face anxiously. "I talked with that lieutenant. Henri, have you decided about tonight? Where will you stay?"

"Don't worry. I'll go home with Pat. It will probably be late when we get through."

She frowned. "And after that?"

I shrugged. "I'll worry about that when the time comes. Right now I'm just trying to get through today! I have to run," I added before she could speak. "We have an anniversary edition to get out, remember?"

"Where have you been?" Morgan stormed as I hurried back to my desk. It was still raining, although not as violently as before, and water dripped from my raincoat into a puddle on the floor.

"At the school, of course. I'm always there on Thursdays."

166

I might as well have told him I had gone to Mars. "I was worried to death! I didn't know where you were. I looked in here to ask you to lunch, and you were gone!" He whisked me into his office, spattering the wall with rain drops. "What was I to think with this, this psychopath on the loose? Henri, you're going to have to be more careful."

I threw my coat on a chair. "Why didn't you just ask Mildred? She always knows where I am."

He pulled me against him. "I don't know anything for sure, except that I love you, Henrietta."

The warm refuge of Morgan's arms was the only security I knew. I wanted to stand there forever, ignoring my problems, hoping they would go away.

Reluctantly, I turned my face aside. "Mildred could walk in, Morgan, or Charlie."

He grinned. "So? Let them!" He gathered my fingers under his chin so that I couldn't pull away. "The lieutenant told me about your picture, who those people were. He really means to locate your elusive Maggie Grey. If you know where she is, you should tell him, Henri."

I pulled away from him. "Why do you say that? You know I don't."

Morgan studied the top of his desk, his hands in his pockets. When he finally spoke, his voice was calm, unemotional, as if he were speaking to a stranger. "Because if you know anything about her, it's important that you tell him." His voice rose. "This Chuckler, whoever he was, he *planned* those murders, all of them! He could still be alive, right here in Raven Rock. And he's after you next, Henrietta."

"Stop it!" I cried. I could feel the tears behind my eyes but I refused to let them flow. "Why are you trying to scare me?"

"Because you're in danger." His hands on my arms were hurting me. "I want you to realize that before it's too late." Abruptly he released me. "Let's accept the obvious, Henri. Someone connected with Essie's committed the Chuckler murders, and that someone is still around."

"I know," I said. "I came to the same conclusion." It was surprising how normal my voice sounded.

"It has to be someone," he went on, "who either roomed or boarded there or was closely connected in some other way—someone we know, Henrietta, someone we trust."

"Don't you know I've thought of that? These people are my friends, Morgan. Almost everyone I know here has had some connection with Essie's, even you!"

He smiled. "That's right. Dad and I took most of our meals at Essie's for a long time after my mother died. She must have fed half the town! Of course, she had more help then, and she was a lot younger." He stared at the floor, a distant look in his eyes, as if he could picture them sitting around the huge dining-room table. "The Waverly sisters were there then, and Howard Lucas. Charlie roomed there, too, for a while before he married."

"Charlie Rogers? Our Charlie? He never mentioned that."

"Well, there's nothing unusual about it," Morgan replied. "It was the only place to stay except for the old hotel, and that wasn't too clean."

"Joyce and Dan were around then, too," I added, "and Seth."

"Seth was away at prep school most of the time," Morgan explained. "He couldn't have been more than sixteen or seventeen."

"All those people, all our friends . . ." I felt a desperate, sinking sensation, as if everything familiar were sliding away. "Morgan, what was it like back then? Can you remember? The people who lived there, ate there, did anything odd take place?"

He picked up a newspaper, slammed it hard against his desk. "Henri, I was seven or eight years old! How can you expect me to remember things like that?"

"I'm sorry. I keep forgetting. It's just that you were here and I wasn't! There's so much I need to find out, so much I don't know. You think you know people, really know them, but you don't. You can't."

His hands dropped to his sides. "Henri, those people back then, they're vague to me now, blank faces, that's all. Except for Maggie, your mother's friend, Maggie Grey. I thought she was beautiful! I liked her, too. She played games with me, teased me." He laughed. "I was lonely, I guess. I used to wish she and Dad would marry, so she could live with us and be my mother."

My face felt like cardboard. I sagged into a chair. "What gave you that idea? Were she and your dad . . . ?"

My reaction went apparently unnoticed as he began rearranging the papers on his desk. "Oh, they dated some," he continued. "They were just good friends, I guess. Nothing came of it. But we saw a lot of Maggie for a while." He smiled. "I guess I was a little in love with her myself!"

"Do you remember when she left?" It was difficult to speak above a whisper.

"What?" He glanced at me sharply, as if he had just remembered I was there.

"I said, do you remember when Maggie Grey left here?"

He shook his head. "No, not exactly. I do remember a peculiar, empty feeling of having lost someone I cared for. I missed her for a while. Dad told me she had gone to live with her parents."

"And had she?" I dared to look him in the eyes.

"Apparently not. Lieutenant Griswold tells me that her mother still lives somewhere in the state. She doesn't know what happened to her either. But whatever happened to Maggie Grey had something to do with the Chuckler murders. It had something to do with you, too, didn't it, Henri?"

I stood on wooden legs. The chair teetered behind me.

Morgan offered a steadying hand. "Henri, you're as pale as a ghost! I'm sorry, I shouldn't have upset you."

I looked into eyes green like mine; at hair fairer, but brown like mine; at a straight nose, a wide mouth, much like my own. I saw them through a distorted blur. My God, had I fallen in love with my brother?

Twenty-eight

"Morgan, it's after three. Pat will be here soon, and we haven't even run off the proofs. Shouldn't we get back to work?" I avoided the hurt look in his eyes as I blindly brushed him aside.

He stepped away from me. "Henri? What is it? Are you sure you're all right?"

"I'm fine, really." I couldn't bear to meet his eyes. "But I do need to get back to work on that feature you wanted on the founding fathers of Raven Rock, or I'll never have it finished in time." For once I was glad for my little cubicle and the privacy it provided, glad for an excuse to pour myself into my work.

Morgan hardly spoke to me for the rest of the day, except for an occasional comment about the copy. Once or twice I felt his eyes on me and would turn to find him staring at me in that same puzzled way.

If Dr. Lawrence had been my mother's lover, he would have been in a position to terminate her pregnancy, but from what I had learned about Maggie Grey I doubted if she had considered that. The two of them had given me a chance at life. Perhaps I should be thankful for that, but at that particular moment I wasn't especially grateful.

Did Morgan's father really believe she had gone to live with her parents? Was he aware of her disappearance? I wondered if he had tried to find her. Perhaps he had been relieved to be rid of her. Did he know more than he admitted? Surely a man in his position would have at least offered financial support. Or would he?

I imagined the distraught Maggie Grey leaving her baby with the Merediths to plead with her lover for help. And he, he . . . A shudder went through me. I couldn't accuse this man of murdering my mother. I had no proof. And what if I was wrong? I had to find out the truth.

A shadow crept over my desk. "Charlie's going out for sandwiches. We're dining in tonight. What'll you have on yours?" It was Pat, pencil poised above a pad. She frowned, peering at me closer. "Hey, what's the matter? You don't really have to tip me if you don't want to! Cheer up!"

I grinned. "Sorry. Just try and pretend I'm not here."

"I know. You're worried about that maniac. I don't blame you. You are staying with me tonight?"

I nodded. "If you can stand me."

"You'll feel better after you're fed." She scribbled on her pad, announcing as she wrote, "One burger with onions! That should keep the boogie man away. And you want fries, don't you?"

The fries were limp and soggy, appropriate for my mood. I nibbled absently as I proofread my copy. It was late, and the office was silent except for the shuffle of papers, the occasional squeak of a chair, and the drip-dripping of the everlasting rain. A long, drawn-out sigh behind me brought my head up with a jerk. "You about through?" Pat leaned on my desk. I abandoned the fries. "Almost. Need some help?" "Would you mind? Mildred was going to read some of this for me, but I see she conveniently forgot." "That's okay. We'll wade through it together. Where's Morgan?"

"Oh, he went over to get some pictures of the haunted house." She rolled her eyes. "And good riddance! Such a mood he's in! Charlie's still here, though," she added, seeing my expression. "And it shouldn't take long with the two of us reading."

We were still reading an hour later. Pat yawned and rummaged in her sweater pocket. "Damn! Wouldn't you know it? I'm out of cigarettes! I don't suppose you smoke?"

"You know I don't have any vices," I bragged. "Maybe Charlie has an extra cigar."

She made a face. "Wonder if the café's still open?"

"Hey, wait a minute! I think Joyce left a pack in my car this morning. I remember seeing them in the seat. It might not be your brand."

"Who cares?" She grabbed my raincoat from its peg. "I'll be back in a minute!"

I started after her. "Wait a minute! I'll go with you. It's dark out there."

She waved me back, brandishing a flashlight. "I'm armed. Just come a runnin' if you hear me yell!"

I sat down and started on another galley, noting that we were almost through. But something was wrong. I let the galleys slide to the floor and, through no will of my own, moved like a zombie toward the back door. A cold blade of fear stabbed through me, making breathing difficult. It was almost as if someone were whispering softly, urgently in my ear. And I knew that danger was near.

"Charlie!" I screamed. A light was on in his office, but no one answered. Trembling, I forced my rock-weighted feet to run, through the narrow back door and into the wet, black void of the parking lot.

I saw them struggling at the car, a sturdy figure in a clown's white mask and Pat, twisting, flailing, fighting for breath, for life against the thing that threatened her.

I must have screamed. Hours later my throat still ached from it. And for a moment time stood still—the two figures in the black rain, and me watching them, unable to move, a still-shot of a bad dream.

Suddenly the grotesque figure released her, hesitated as if deciding what to do, then bolted across the parking lot. Pat stumbled, sagged, sliding against the car. I reached her as she dropped to the wet asphalt, gasping, clutching at her throat.

She fought me as I tried to pick her up. Her dark hair was plastered against her face, her eyes wild. The broken flashlight rolled at my feet.

"It's all right now, Pat! It's me, it's Henri. He's gone now. You're going to be okay." Drunkenly we stumbled toward the building.

Two yellow headlights slashed the darkness; a car door slammed; running footsteps closed in on us—Morgan!

"It was the Chuckler! He tried to choke her!" I answered his unspoken question. Without a word, he scooped Pat in his arms, carried her inside. Together we removed her shoes, her raincoat, rubbed her with rough towels until her skin turned red.

Morgan grabbed the telephone and began to dial. "Get her something hot to drink! I'll call the police. She'll need a doctor, too."

The coffee pot was empty, and only a dusting of grounds remained in the bottom of the can. It had been a busy week. I turned to Morgan. "We're out of coffee. Do you have any more?"

"Did I hear someone say, 'coffee'? How's this for service?" Charlie ambled in with a cardboard carton holding three large cups. "I couldn't remember how everyone liked it, so it's all black. Hope that's okay?" His words dwindled as he noticed Pat shivering in a chair with Morgan's coat around her. His glance took in Morgan's anxious face, my bedraggled appearance.

"Someone tried to choke Pat in the parking lot," I explained, taking the drinks from him. "I called for you but you didn't answer."

Charlie's face turned pale as he slumped beside Pat's chair. "Oh, my God! Are you all right? I only went next door to the café for coffee. We didn't have any, and it looked like it was going to be a long night." He covered his face with his hands. "I'm sorry . . . so sorry."

"Charlie, don't!" Morgan said. "It wasn't your fault. I wasn't here either. I should never have left."

"It probably wouldn't have made any difference," I said. "He ran when he saw me, before he could do any real harm."

Pat sipped at the hot liquid. "This feels good. Thank you, Charlie." She smiled, a little color coming back into her face.

The police arrived soon after that, followed by Dr. Lawrence. As I talked with the detective, he examined Pat, prescribing a tranquilizer and medication for her throat. "She'll be sore and hoarse for a few days," he told us, "but other than that, she's going to be fine. Thank heavens you got to her in time, Henri! A few seconds later, and it might have been a different story." He seemed so kind, so concerned, the perfect picture of the warm, caring, family physician. It was hard to believe he had ever done anything cruel or unkind.

"Dad, I think you'd better look at Henri, too." Morgan studied me seriously. "She's had a pretty rough time of it."

"No! Thank you, I'm fine." I moved away from them. I couldn't bear to have Dr. Lawrence touch me. "I really don't need anything except to be left alone!"

Morgan and his father exchanged glances. "I understand," the doctor said. Morgan didn't say anything, but I could see that he didn't understand. He probably never would.

"I know you're all eager to get home," Lieutenant Griswold began. "If I could just speak with Miss Meredith for a few minutes, I believe we can call it a night."

I followed him into Morgan's office, where we had held our earlier conversation that afternoon. I felt at least ten years older.

"I don't have to tell you how serious this is," he explained. He hesitated, as if trying to choose the right words. "You realize this Chuckler, or whoever he is, was not after your friend tonight?"

I leaned against the desk, feeling the worn, ink-stained blotter under my hands. "What? What do you mean?"

"I *mean* that this strangler thought it was you out there." His voice dropped, taking on an urgent tone. "He was waiting, you see, waiting for you. You and Pat Saxon are about the same size. She had on your raincoat, went to your car . . ." He watched as the realization struck me. "He didn't intend to kill Pat, Miss Meredith. He meant to kill you."

"But why? Why? What have I done? I don't understand." I stood, facing him. "Don't you have any idea who it could be? Did you find anything outside?"

He sighed. "This time he didn't have time to leave a calling card, and, of course, there were no footprints on the asphalt. But, yes, we do have an idea, and with your cooperation, hopefully we can find out for sure."

I stared at his rain-splashed overcoat. There was a button missing, the second from the top. "What do you want me to do?"

"Good!" He clapped his hands together. "First of all, we want you to try to get a good night's sleep. We'll have a man on duty at the Saxon's. I don't think there will be any trouble tonight. Then, tomorrow, I want you to drive to Shannon to your grandmother's. Spend the weekend there, away from here, away from everyone. Let things cool down a little."

"My grandmother? You haven't told anyone, have you? About who I am?"

"No one knows that except myself and a few other police officials. I can assure you your secret is safe with us."

"But I don't want my grandmother to know about all of this. She'll wonder why I . . ."

He smiled. "How good an actress are you? Tell her you have a long weekend and needed some country air. I've already talked with Mr. Lawrence. You needn't come in tomorrow."

"Does *he* know where I'm going?"

He frowned. "Of course not. I told him you'll be staying with friends in the city." He paced across the office, his shoes leaving damp, dark spots on the floor.

177

"And then what?" I asked. "I have to come back some time."

"Yes, and that's going to be the most difficult part." He paused in his pacing, studied me silently. "It will take a lot of courage on your part, and absolute silence. You can't tell anyone, not even your best friend. If you do, you'll blow the whole thing, maybe even your life."

"Blow *what*? What is it I'm supposed to do?"

"We want you to stay in Honeysuckle House, alone. Oh, we'll have someone watching you day and night, although I don't believe he's going to try anything in daylight. No, it's going to happen at night, when he thinks no one is watching. Only we'll be watching, Miss Meredith. Someone will be with you all the time, inside Honeysuckle House."

I shook my head. "You don't know my friends. They'll never allow me to stay there after tonight! They'll insist . . ."

"Then *you* insist even more. Play the whole thing down. Tell them we think it was a Halloween prank. Tell them anything but the truth." His eyes challenged mine. "It's a lot to ask, but if we're going to put a stop to this reign of terror, it's the only way. Think you can do it?"

I shrugged. "Do I have any choice?"

Twenty-nine

"You don't mean you're going to stay in Honeysuckle House alone?" Seth asked. We were sitting at Essie's long dining-room table the night of my return from Shannon. There had been no way I could have refused her invitation to supper when I stopped by to tell her I was back. And so I had stayed, and now I was trying to convince Seth and the others that I would be safe staying alone in the cottage. It was not an easy thing to do.

"Why, I just won't have it! You'll stay right here, after what happened to that Saxon girl!" Essie waved her fork in midair. "It's not safe for a girl to be alone."

I broke open a biscuit, smothered it in honey. "Pat was really more frightened than she was hurt. The police think it was a Halloween joke."

"But that's ridiculous! How can they possible believe that after what happened to your kitten?" Howard Lucas spooned gravy over his grits and mixed them together with an expert twist of his fork.

"I haven't even had a chance to tell you I'm sorry about the kitten," Seth whispered beside me. "When you think you're ready for another, just let me know, and I'll check the nearest cotton patch."

Miss Carrie smiled across from me. "Better take another biscuit, Maggie. Butter it while it's hot."

I glanced at her sharply, but she was looking down at her plate, toying with her food.

"That's not Maggie, Carrie," her sister pointed out. "That's Henrietta."

"Oh!" Miss Carrie giggled. "Did I call you Maggie? But you do look like Maggie, dear. Are you related?"

I smiled and shook my head, stuffing my mouth full of ham. The idea of being bait for a crazed killer had made me lose my appetite, but eating was the only way I could avoid answering questions. I chewed the bite for a long time and kept my eyes on my plate, hoping they would change the topic of conversation.

Miss Carrie lifted a fork to her mouth and put it down again. "Such a sweet girl Maggie was, remember, Cora? I was fond of her. Wonder why she never . . ."

"Well, Henri, how were things in the city?" Essie asked. "Did you have a nice visit with your friends?"

"Oh yes," I lied. "It's always nice to see old friends." I ate another biscuit.

When the meal was finally over, I hurriedly helped Essie clear the table, eager to escape to Honeysuckle House and telephone Lieutenant Griswold. He had told me to let him know as soon as I got back in town. But it was difficult getting away from Essie, and even more difficult trying to pry myself loose from the roomers who wanted to hear all about the incident on Halloween.

A bony hand clutched at me as I returned from carrying dishes into the kitchen. Miss Carrie lurked behind the swinging door. "There's something I've been meaning to tell you," she whispered. "You seem interested in finding out about Maggie Grey . . ." Her blue eyes darted from side to side.

"Yes, yes I am!" I let her pull me into a corner.

"We never saw her after she left here, you know," Miss Carrie continued. "But a good while after that, several months or so, I saw a letter from Maggie here on the hall table, at least it had her name in the left-hand corner." She smiled. "I thought you'd like to know."

I put my hand on her arm. Her wrist was no bigger than a child's. Hannah's would have made two of it! "Do you remember who the letter was for, Miss Carrie?"

A vague look came into her eyes, and she edged away from me, slipping into the hall.

"Miss Carrie!" I called. "Can't you . . ."

"Oh, there you are." It was Seth. "Henri, I wish you'd change your mind about staying at the cottage. But if you insist, then at least let me go over with you, just to see if everything's okay."

It seemed to be the only way out, so I agreed. Seth was quiet during the brief walk to the cottage, but as we approached the front door, he spoke, sighing as if he were reluctant to begin. "I'm sorry you're having such a hard time of it here, Henri, especially since I'm responsible for your living in Honeysuckle House." His voice was heavy with sadness. "I wish it could have worked out, but sometimes people and places are not what they seem. I believe you're in real danger here, Henrietta. I want you to leave, soon, before something terrible happens."

People are not always as they seem. I pondered Seth's words as I lay awake that night in my room upstairs. He was trying to warn me about someone, but who?

Down in my darkened living room a policeman sat on guard. Now and then I could hear the wicker chair creak with his weight. Outside, concealed by darkness and trees, another policeman waited, waited for a faceless someone to make his last mistake. Soon, perhaps, it would be all over, and I would at last see the face of my persecutor and learn the reason behind this madness. Yet, as eager as I was to end my ordeal, I dreaded to learn the truth. Which of my friends hated me enough to try to take my life? Could it be Dan or Joyce attempting to rebury some dreadful secret from the past? Or Dr. Lawrence, struggling to survive as the gallant town physician? Perhaps even Charlie, who had been conspicuously absent when the Chuckler had struck. Essie, Seth, the Waverly sisters, even Morgan— one of them was not as he seemed. One of them was living in a normal, human shell, while crumbling away inside.

The house was still. I had left my bedroom door partially open, as I had been instructed. No light burned. At the first hint of an intruder, I was to turn on my bedside lamp to alert the policeman in the woods. Poor man! I hoped he had brought a thermos of something hot. November is a cold month in the mountains, and I could hear the wind rising in the tall pines outside my window as their feathery branches lashed against the roof. It was going to be a long night.

I awoke a little disappointed that nothing had happened, yet relieved that I had not been threatened. Then I realized it was still dark. I had only been asleep a few hours. But something had wakened me, not a noise, not a touch, something else. What was it? I sniffed. A fragrance! A man's fragrance, cologne or after-shave with a heavy, oriental scent. I had smelled it before, recently. I stiffened, hardly daring to breathe. The scent was overpowering, close, somewhere in the room!

I opened my eyes, let them become accustomed to the night. There at the foot of my bed, a dark figure stood. It moved!

Silently in the darkness I reached for the lamp and pressed the switch, screaming at the same time.

When I opened my eyes, Lieutenant Griswold was shaking me. I had closed them instinctively when I turned on the light, afraid of what I might see. I had heard footsteps bolting down the stairs, another set running up, and the scuffle that ensued. Now all was quiet except for my incoherent sobbing and the detective's soothing voice.

"It's all right, Miss Meredith. It's over now. We have him downstairs. He won't bother you again."

"Have who? Who is it?"

"Don't you know? Didn't you see him?"

"I was afraid to look," I confessed.

"It was Seth Honeycutt, Miss Meredith, the one we suspected it might be." His words came like a whiplash, in spite of his gentle voice.

The detective turned his back as I tossed the covers aside, but his modest actions were unnecessary. I had felt vulnerable enough without waiting for a murderer in my night clothes. I had not bothered to undress before going to bed. I hurried downstairs to find Seth slumped in a chair, his face toward the wall, his hands cuffed together. The second policeman stood guard over him while they waited for the patrol car to arrive.

I stood in the doorway. "Oh, Seth, why?"

He looked at me, his dark eyes filled with misery. "I wasn't going to hurt you, Henri. I didn't mean . . . please don't hate me!" He turned his face away and was silent. When they took him away, I was glad.

"Do you feel like coming with me over to Essie's?" Lieutenant Griswold bundled into his coat. "This is

183

going to break her heart, and I don't mind telling you, I'm not looking forward to telling her.''

"Do you think I should?" I asked. "After all, if it weren't for me, this wouldn't have happened. She didn't want me here to begin with.''

"I've called Dr. Lawrence, but he won't be able to stay. She'll need someone young and strong to lean on. The Waverly sisters won't be much help.''

"I think she'd prefer them to me tonight," I said. "She's always been so kind to me, and now this!''

He shook his head. "Don't kid yourself. From what I've heard, Seth has always been a problem. When he was younger, they tell me she had to send him to prep school to keep him out of trouble.''

"Seth? I can't believe it," I said. "It's hard to believe Seth could hurt anyone. He's always been so pleasant, so gentle.''

He wrapped a giant scarf around his neck, pulled a hat over his ears. "You saw him, didn't you? He was here, in this house! What other proof do you need?" He carefully worked his big hands into thick gloves. "Besides, there are other things, things I haven't told you. Seth Honeycutt dated that Tatum girl, the carhop who was murdered. And he used to babysit for Ann Taylor. He could easily have sneaked away from that school long enough to do what he did. And, of course, he was home most weekends. We just put two and two together." He shrugged. "A little late, perhaps, but in time to help you. So don't you worry about being to blame. There's only one person to blame, and that's Seth Honeycutt!''

Essie was wearing the same green housedress she had worn at supper. It seemed almost as if she were expecting us. I think she must have thought the lieutenant was checking to see if she was all right. "Why, come on in, Officer! I just couldn't get to sleep," she explained, "so I thought I'd work on my quilt a while." Her eyes widened when she saw me. "Henrietta! What is it? Is anything wrong?"

When we told her, she was almost stoic. "You have the wrong person, Lieutenant. Seth wouldn't do that. Seth wouldn't hurt anyone. He's good. Seth's good!" Finally she began to cry silently and obediently let me lead her upstairs to bed, where Dr. Lawrence gave her a shot to make her sleep.

I stayed with her all night. In the morning I explained to the roomers what had happened and helped them to get breakfast in a slipshod way. Dr. Lawrence stopped by again on his way to the hospital, surprised that I was still there. "You go on home and get some sleep," he instructed me. "I'll call one of the neighbors to stay with Essie."

I left, but I didn't go back to the cottage. Instead I went to *The Register* office to tell everyone the joyful news, that now I could begin to lead a normal life. Only somehow it seemed a hollow victory.

Thirty

I called Lieutenant Griswold that afternoon to ask if
Seth had admitted anything more, if there had been
a link between my mother's disappearance and the
Chuckler murders. But Seth wasn't talking, the detective told me. Or, if he was, the lieutenant didn't want
me to know about it.

As the day wore on, sleepiness dragged at me. It
became an effort to press the keys of my typewriter;
the print on my copy blurred before my eyes.

Morgan stopped by my desk. "Go on home, Henrietta. You put up a good fight. Now it's over. Get
some sleep." A smile crept across his face. "Just this
once, maybe I can manage the society news."

It was a noble concession. I thanked him and left,
but I didn't want to return to Honeysuckle House, not
yet. My feet took me to Essie's, although my selfish
heart rebelled. I had to reassure myself that her mettle
would see her through this nightmare, that she wouldn't
hate me for it.

I found her puttering in the kitchen. "You don't
have to do this," I said. "No one expects you to cook
tonight."

She slashed at a potato. "Gives me something to do. I've worked all my life. I'm used to it."

"Essie." I put my hand on her shoulder. "About Seth. I feel so sorry, so very sorry."

She wiped an eye with the back of her hand. "He's not guilty, Henrietta. He's done nothing!" Her face was drawn and brooding. "Seth's always been so good to me. He's all I have. They're wrong. I told them they were wrong."

I didn't know what to say. I wanted to comfort her, but my words were empty. I couldn't defend Seth, not even for Essie. "Are you going to be all right?" I asked.

She plucked at her apron as she spoke. "They'll find out they're wrong," she muttered. "They'll see."

I wondered.

I had been through a lot to learn a little. I still didn't know what had happened to my mother and why. Nor was I certain about my father's identity. Because of me, a friend had almost been killed, another arrested, and Essie would have to live with heartbreak.

I was beginning to learn a little about heartbreak, too. I lived with it each time I looked at Morgan and saw the pain in his eyes. He avoided me whenever possible, spoke rarely. As soon as I learned what had happened to my mother, I would leave Raven Rock, leave Morgan. Until then I knew I could not get him out of my mind. I thought of him constantly, was thinking of him that night when he knocked so insistently at my door. I was up to my elbows in soapsuds from doing my weekly laundry, and it took me a few minutes to get to the door.

"You scared me to death!" I said as he barged in, bringing the cold air with him.

187

"Damn it, Henrietta, I can't take it anymore! I've had enough of this foolishness! What's the matter with you? Do you enjoy acting like this?"

His ears were red from the cold. His coat was buttoned crooked. He tried to unwind his muffler and succeeded in getting it tangled around his arm. I began to laugh. I guess I must have needed it. Morgan, watching me, grew more and more testy.

I stopped laughing as suddenly as I had begun. He stood there with a sad little smile on his face. "It's really not very funny, is it, Henrietta?"

"No, it isn't." I wanted so much to touch him. "I'm sorry."

"I thought I meant something to you. I know I did. And now there's this distance, this coldness between us. Why?"

"I can't tell you." I turned away from him and walked to the window where the draperies were drawn against the night.

"And I'm supposed to accept that and ask no more questions. Is that it?"

I didn't answer.

"Is that it?" In two steps he was beside me, spinning me around to face him.

"It's because of your father!" I cried.

He frowned. "My father? What does he have to do with it?"

I touched his hand. "Everything. Remember when you told me he dated Maggie Grey? You said you wanted them to marry?"

He nodded, still puzzled.

"Maggie Grey was my mother, Morgan. I have reason to believe you could be my half-brother."

"You can't be serious!" His look was incredulous. "Tell me you aren't serious, Henri. That's ridiculous, impossible!"

"No it isn't, Morgan. They were together at the right time, the right place. Look at us—eyes, hair, coloring, even our features are something alike, enough alike to be brother and sister."

He grinned. "But your ears don't stick out." Gingerly he lifted the hair over my ear as if to make sure.

I shoved his hand away. "Stop it, Morgan! It's not funny."

He frowned. "No, it isn't. Who told you this, Henri? Did you hear this from your mother?"

"Of course not! How could I? I don't even remember my mother. I don't know where she is."

"Is that why you came here to Raven Rock, to find your mother?"

"Yes. As you can see, it hasn't done much good."

"It's been a long time, Henri. A lot can happen in twenty-two years."

"Something terrible happened to her! I feel it. I know it. People are holding things back. Someone is hiding something."

"Your mother could be living in a vine-covered cottage with a husband and ten children by now. Why will you think the worst?"

"Because," I said, "I know. And Miss Carrie told me she saw a letter from her several months after she left here."

He groaned. "That was years ago."

"Yes, but why didn't someone tell me about it? Why did they keep it a secret? They said they never heard from her again!"

"They probably forgot," Morgan explained. "And consider the source, Henri. You can't believe everything Miss Carrie says."

"I believe my mother sent that letter," I told him. "And someone here knew where she went. I believe she meant to come back for me and something happened to prevent it."

"And you think my father would have abandoned you, either of you, if you had been his child? You don't know him very well."

"That's why I can be objective," I argued.

"We'll see," Morgan answered. "We'll ask him together."

"Why can't you ask him? Why do I have to be there?"

"Because this was *your* idea, Henrietta. No, you come with me, the sooner the better. We'll get rid of that notion once and for all!"

"All right," I agreed. "When?"

"He's on duty at the hospital now. It will have to be tomorrow night." He touched me lightly on the chin. "You won't chicken out on me, will you?"

Before I could answer, he kissed me briefly but thoroughly before letting me go. "Does that make you feel sisterly?" he asked, slamming the door behind him.

Thirty-one

That night I had the dream again. My mother was cutting flowers in a garden; I moved toward her at a somnambulistic pace, wanting to be near her, to touch her. But instead of giving me a welcoming smile, she drew away from me, frantically motioned me back, until the fear that was in her transferred to me. I began to run!

When I woke, the light, sweet scent of honeysuckle lingered in the room. The dream was obviously meant to have significance: my mother cutting flowers, the drone of bees, the terror in her eyes. Was Maggie Grey trying to warn me about Seth Honeycutt? If so, she was a day late. Seth Honeycutt was safely locked away. I shuddered to think how I had trusted him, had even felt affection for the man.

The dream brought me thoroughly awake. I had gone to bed early, to compensate for the sleep I had missed the night before. I had slept less than two hours, yet I felt wide awake, fidgety, and I knew that it would be useless to remain in bed.

I was enjoying a late snack of soup and crackers when the phone rang. It was not yet eleven and most of my friends knew I hardly ever went to bed before midnight, so the late call didn't surprise me. But there was something else that alarmed me, a presage in the jangle of the bell.

"Miss Meredith?" The voice was not familiar. "This is Ruth Whitaker, Hannah's mother. Is my daughter with you?"

"Why, no, no, she isn't! Mrs. Whitaker, what's wrong? Has Hannah run away?"

"I don't know." There was a tremble in her voice. "I just got home from my shift at the mill, and she was gone. Her bed's empty!"

"Do you know how long she's been gone?"

"No, my husband was asleep when I came in. He didn't get off work until afternoon. I . . . we quarreled last night, and I guess Hannah overheard us. I'm afraid that's why she's gone. Her father's out looking for her now," she sobbed.

"Have you checked with the Saxons?" I asked. "She could be staying with Mary Faye."

"I called there first," she said. "She's not there. Mary Faye hasn't seen her since school let out."

"Mrs. Whitaker, I think you should call the police. It sounds like Hannah never came home from school. I'll call Joyce McDonald and see if she knows anything, but I'm sure she would have called you if Hannah were with her."

I dialed Joyce's number, letting the phone ring several times before I remembered that it was their daughter's birthday and they were driving over to the college she attended to take her out to dinner. Joyce had shown me the watch they were giving her when she had been staying with me the week before. Hannah couldn't be with them! Then where could she be?

Where would a sensitive, ten-year-old go when she was unhappy?

To a place where she had been happy, of course! A place that was special to her—Morgan's cabin! I recalled the child's affection for the place, her desire to go back again and again.

I hadn't thought to ask Ruth Whitaker if Hannah's bike was gone, but I was almost certain that it was. She had probably cycled to the cabin directly from school, while it was light and sunny and she was still feeling resentful and very, very brave. Now it would be dark and cold, too late to ride home alone.

I called the Lawrence home and explained to Alice the necessity of finding Morgan.

"I'm sorry, Henri. Morgan left here hours ago. Said he had several errands to run. I gave him a cake to take by Essie's, poor thing!" She hesitated. "Do you really think that child is out at that lake alone?"

"I don't know. I'm going to drive out there and see. Will you tell Morgan when you see him, in case I miss him at Essie's?"

"Of course. Would you like me to go with you, Henri?"

"I think it might be better if I went alone. I don't know what kind of state she's in."

"I hope you find her," Alice said. "And if you need to get in the cabin, the key's on a nail under the second step."

Essie's voice sounded old and tired when she answered the phone.

"Essie? It's Henri," I said. "I hope I didn't wake you."

"I couldn't get to sleep. It's useless to try."

"I wouldn't have bothered you this late, but I'm trying to find Morgan," I explained. "Hannah Whitaker has disappeared, and I think she might have gone to his cabin. Alice said I might find him at your house."

"He was here, Henri, but he left ages ago. He didn't say where he was going. Is Hannah the child you're so fond of? Why would she do a thing like that?"

"It's a long story," I said, "but I have to drive out to the lake and see if she's there. If Morgan should call, will you tell him where I've gone?"

"You're not going out there alone? Why not let the police check it out?"

"It's just a hunch, Essie. I'd hate to send them off on a wild goose chase. And if she is there, she's probably frightened to death already without being hauled home by strangers. Hannah knows me; she trusts me. Besides, I feel partially responsible."

"Poor little tyke! Have you told her parents you're going?"

"No. I don't want to get their hopes up in case I don't find her."

There was a pause. "I hope you do, Henri. But do be careful." Her voice was stronger, more spirited than it had been earlier. "Everything will work out all right," she told me confidently. I smiled. It looked like Essie was going to get through this after all!

I noticed by the courthouse clock that it was almost midnight as I passed through the center of town. The desolate streets were washed in moonlight. My uneasiness grew, and as the yellow headlights pierced the darkness of the lonely country road, an awareness of impending danger to Hannah settled around me like a black, heavy cloak. I dreaded what I might find. I pressed down on the accelerator as I neared the lake, hoping to get there in time to prevent . . . what? I had visions of Hannah huddled, freezing, on the cabin steps, stumbling in the darkness into the icy waters of the lake, being pursued by some faceless figure in the night. The little car bumped and slithered over the ragged road to the cabin, where I brought it to a shaking halt and threw open my door to the cold night, fighting to shake off the depression that smothered me.

Through the windows of the cabin came the flickering, orange glow of firelight, and in front of the massive stone fireplace a little figure hunched before the blaze.

I opened the door and stood there silently for a minute. I didn't want to frighten her away. "Hannah? It's Henri. Are you all right?"

She turned, her small, round face peeking out from a cave of blankets. "Henri! Did you come to take me home?"

I smiled. "Are you ready?"

She nodded, rising drowsily to her feet. "Are they very mad, Henri? My parents? I guess they're about ready to kill me!"

"They're worried sick about you, Hannah. Your parents care about you. They love you." I heard a car pull up outside, footsteps on the gravel. Morgan had gotten my message. "Why did you come out here, Hannah? How did you get in?"

She yawned. "Because I like it. And I knew where the key was. I found some stuff to eat, but I had an awful time getting a fire started. It was cold out here, and scary by myself. And it was too dark to come home. I'm glad you came, Henri."

I put my arms around her, blanket and all. "I'm glad, too. You really had us worried, but running away isn't the best way to solve our problems. I guess you know that now."

"Not necessarily." It was Essie standing behind us, her face set and hard. "You should have run while you had the chance, Henrietta. I warned you. How many times did I warn you? But you wouldn't listen, would you? You had to stir up old ashes, drag the dead back from their graves!"

"Essie? What . . ." I half-smiled, thinking she was joking, but when I saw her eyes I knew the truth that had evaded me for so long. All the bitterness and malice that had been festering in Essie Honeycutt was concentrated in her eyes—and her eyes were on me!

In that frantic moment I remembered Mom's warning, the words she spoke to me before she died: *You have your whole life ahead of you. Don't look back.* But I had. I had stepped into a nightmare, and I had taken Hannah with me.

Thirty-two

I made an abrupt move toward the door, pulling Hannah with me, but Essie stepped in my way. I was amazed at how solid she was, strong and solid. I had never noticed it before. Then I saw the small, gray revolver. The barrel gleamed with a dull, metallic glow in the dim cabin light. She jangled my car keys in my face. "You wouldn't get very far without these!" She laughed, dropping them in her coat pocket. The faint, depraved chuckle coming from the lips of someone I had liked and trusted brought tears to my eyes. It was the same laugh I had heard on the phone.

"Essie, you're sick. I don't think you realize what you're doing." I reached out instinctively. Her hand came down in a streak of gray, striking my wrist with the gun. I heard the bone crack.

Hannah screamed, clutching me tightly as I cried out in pain. I fought back the tears, the nausea. She wanted to see me cry. "How can you do this to this child?" I screamed. "Has she ever done anything to you? If you're going to hurt me, there's nothing I can do about it, but you'll have to kill me before I'll let you harm Hannah!"

She smiled. "That's exactly what I had in mind."

"Let her go, Essie! She's ten years old. She's terrified. Can't you see that?" Now I was begging.

Essie folded her arms, waved the revolver carelessly. "That's too bad, Henrietta. I didn't force her to come out here. I didn't plan this little outing. Funny how things work out, isn't it? I couldn't have arranged a more convenient setting. I've been waiting for this chance since that mix-up on Halloween."

"It was you all the time, wasn't it? The snapshot, the kitten, the clown that night at the cabin, and then Pat. You could have killed her!"

She shrugged. "I thought it was you, Henrietta."

"But why, Essie? What have I ever done to you? Why do you hate me so?"

"I don't hate you, Henrietta. I tried to warn you, over and over. I didn't want to kill you, believe me, I didn't."

The pain came in waves now. I breathed deeply. "Then why? Why?"

"I know who you are," she said. "I suspected from the first. Then, when that photograph turned up, I knew for sure. So much like her, you are. And now you can die like she did!"

"My mother! You killed my mother!" If it hadn't been for Hannah, I would have thrown myself upon her, regardless of the gun. "Why, Essie? Why?"

She regarded me coldly. "She was a troublemaker, like you. Stupid girl! She thought Seth killed those women. She was going to the police." Her eyes glinted dangerously. "She thought Seth was the Chuckler. Can you imagine, Seth?"

My arm clung to Hannah like a dead, unfeeling weight. My injured wrist hung throbbing at my side. Now everything was falling into place. Essie was delirious with madness, her eyes feverish. She was deranged, this woman who held us in her power. We were dealing with someone who had gone beyond the edge of reason, someone who had killed repeatedly and would not hesitate to murder again. Hannah had stopped crying and stood stiffly against me, staring at the terror that threatened us.

Essie nudged me with a gun. "I'll have to urge you to do a little writing for me, if you please." She spoke without expression. "Over there, sit down at the table, both of you." She tossed me my pocketbook. "Find a scrap of paper, anything will do, and a pencil. Hurry!"

I scrambled in the depths of the bag, pretending to search for the items, until she grabbed it from me in desperation and emptied the contents on the table.

"Now," she said, as I sat with pad and pencil before me, "we wouldn't want anyone to get the wrong impression, so you'll just write a little message to keep things straight." She laughed. "Your last piece of reporting, Henrietta, so make it good."

Hannah's lips trembled. "Don't do it, Henri! She's going to kill us."

Essie took a deep breath. "I want you to tell them," she measured her words, "that you alone are responsible for the things that have happened recently: the kitten's death, the notes, the attack on Pat, everything."

"This is ridiculous!" I protested. "They're not going to believe that."

"Write it!" she barked, leveling the gun at Hannah's head. "And write it fast. I don't think the police will think to look here for the child, but I want to be gone if they do."

"Alice Lawrence knows where I am," I said. "And Morgan should be here any minute, as soon as he gets my message."

She patted my shoulder, a mockery of her old self. "Oh, I took care of that for you, dear. I called Alice after I talked with you and told her not to bother Morgan, that you had decided to let the police check it out and wouldn't be going after all." Her smile was smug. "And, of course, I thanked her for the cake. Did you know she sent me a cake? People are so thoughtful, aren't they?"

She watched as I wrote the words she had instructed in stiff, bold letters on the page. "One more thing," she added, "don't forget to tell them how you lured Seth to your room."

I gasped. "What?"

"Oh, I know you invited him there. I've seen how you've been looking at him, encouraging him with your charms, just like the others!" Her voice rose. "Well, I protected him from those other women, and I'll protect him from you!"

I sighed. "Why would I invite a man to my room with a policeman sitting downstairs?"

"How should I know? Unless it was a trap to have him arrested. You suspected Seth, didn't you?"

"No, Essie, I didn't. And I have no idea why he was in my room, believe me. But Seth's a grown man. Surely you must expect him to have some romance in his life, some girl he cares for."

"Shut up!" she shrieked. "There's no girl good enough for Seth. They're all bad, wicked. Seth will never marry, not as long as I have breath in me."

"Why?" I was stalling for time, and she knew it.

"Never mind, just write what I tell you." She read what I had written and nodded approvingly. "Now, tell them you've been suffering from headaches, blackouts. You're compelled to do things you later regret.

Tell them you killed Hannah during one of your spells, and you can't live with yourself any longer."

"I can't say that!" I sobbed. "I can't!"

The gun was pressed into Hannah's temple. "Yes, you can, and you will. You're a writer, aren't you?"

I picked up the pencil, my body clammy with perspiration. My hand shook as I wrote.

"I think we'll leave the note here in the cabin." She spoke as casually as if she were planning tomorrow's menu. "They'll find your car outside and your bodies down at the lake, out of earshot of the other cabins. Although I doubt if anyone's around on a night like this." She tugged at my arm, pulling me toward the door. Hannah followed, trailing the blanket, her eyes dazed.

I wondered which of us she would kill first. I hoped it would be me. Maybe, if I made it difficult enough, Hannah could slip away, hide in the darkness until help came. I tried to communicate this message to her, but Essie came between us, trampling on the blanket that trailed along the ground. "Throw that thing down! It's in the way."

"Please, Essie. She's cold." She didn't answer, but she let her keep the blanket. Maybe she was saving her energy for the kill.

We plodded over the rugged path to the lake with only the moon for light. The rush of the falls pulsed against the rocks with its dreary, chilling roar. Soon we would see the dark glint of the water. Soon we would die.

"They'll never believe I killed Hannah," I said. "Don't you know that? They'll know you were here. If Seth knew what you were doing, he would hate you, Essie. Do you think this is what he wants? Do you?"

Her breathing was jagged. "No one knows I came here tonight. I made sure they didn't see me leave, and I left the phone off the hook so no one would call and wake the others. For all they'll know, I've been in my room asleep all night." She laughed. "Now they'll believe me! Now they'll know Seth couldn't have done all those things."

"He should be very proud of you," I said.

She didn't say anything more until we came in sight of the huge, black rock, looming like a sinister vulture at the top of the falls. "There's your tombstone!" she said, pointing to the rock. "The family graveyard. Come and join your mother."

Her words knocked the breath from me. "My mother? She's here?"

"Ironic, isn't it? We came here together that night. She had written that she was coming, asked me to meet her bus. We drove out here to talk, she thought. She was a foolish girl, your mother. I had intended to kill her earlier, but she got away from me, went to the city." She shoved us in front of her on the trail. "Of course, I didn't know that then, didn't know where she was, and didn't really care. She was gone, and that was that. I was willing to leave well enough alone. But then she sent that letter. There was something she had to tell me, she said." Essie snickered. "I'll bet she regretted that!"

"But why?" I asked. "Why did you want to kill her?"

"I should think that's obvious! All that shameless carrying on! Well, it caught up with her when she found out she was pregnant. Your mother was a slut! Men around her all the time. Seth, too. As young as he was, she had him wrapped around her little finger— she and that Nell Gordon, sunbathing out in the yard in those skimpy suits, and he not yet out of his teens!

I sent him away to school, but it was too late. The damage had been done!"

Oh, my poor mother! My poor, unsuspecting mother. She had trusted this woman as I had, had believed she was her friend. I looked at the ravenlike rock that had been my mother's grave marker for more than twenty years and was determined it would not be mine—or Hannah's. From somewhere strength and calmness flowed into me, transfusing me with the courage to do what I must. "Oh, wait!" I leaned down, grabbed my shoe.

"What is it?" Essie drew up close behind me. "Don't try any tricks with me. I'd just as soon shoot you now and get it over with."

"My shoe's coming off. Just let me fix it." I snatched the trailing corner of Hannah's blanket, jerked it up-ward and threw it over Essie's bewildered face, shoving her backward on the path. I was taking a chance, gambling our lives in those few, brief seconds, but what did we have to lose?

Essie cried out, thrashing in the darkness. We left her writhing there, a screaming mound of anguish, and ran away from the path and into the black woods, where each footstep gave us away. In the darkness I hadn't been able to tell if Essie had been hurt in the scuffle, but I knew she still had the gun. She also had the keys to both cars.

Thirty-three

"She's coming, Henri! She'll kill us!" Hannah sobbed. We could hear Essie crashing about in the underbrush looking for us.

"We'll have to separate," I whispered. "She can't chase both of us."

"No!" She clung to me, shivering. "I want to stay with you."

"Hannah, we have to separate. It's our only chance." I gripped her cold hand in mine. "Now listen, we'll both make it out of here if we don't panic. Go back to the cabin, but don't go in. Follow the driveway out to the road, and start walking toward town. Wave down the first car that passes!" I hugged her briefly. "Can you do that?"

"Uh-huh." Her tears were wet on my face. "But what about you?"

"I'll go the other way, toward the lake. Don't worry, she won't catch me. I'll hide somewhere until help comes. Now remember, be quiet and be careful. Stay on the side of the road." I gave her a little shove, and she was gone, slipping away like a shadow in the darkness.

I plunged toward the lake, branches clawing at my face, tearing at my clothes. I slipped on unseen rocks, stumbled over roots, and with every step I could hear her stalking me—her movements an echo of my own.

The ground descended into a veil of mist, obscuring all but the dark shapes of trees. I smelled the stream before I heard it, gushing beneath the fog. The dark, dank odor of it enveloped me, and I knew I must cross it, the same stream I had tumbled into on that first afternoon at Morgan's cabin, that afternoon so long ago. I stripped off my socks and shoes, bundled them in my coat and held it over my head. The water was icy and swift, but it only came to my thighs. I crossed slowly, blindly feeling each step of the way, and pulled myself up on the opposite side to crouch shivering in the mud.

I heard Essie hesitate on the other side, her cry at the first shock of cold water, and the splashing as she waded across.

I forced dry shoes on sodden feet, one hand useless from pain, the other shaking so I could hardly hold it still, and then continued my frenzied flight from a nightmare that seemed as if it would never cease.

The lake lay before me, smoking fog, a secretive fog that curled in wispy tendrils over the bare November earth. Essie would expect me to run toward the road, toward town. I reached for a stone at my feet and threw it in that direction. I heard her wheezing, lumbering behind me and stood under the spicy branches of a giant cedar as she turned and lunged toward the sound. I knew that my sanctuary was temporary. Soon Essie would discover she had been misled, and even now the fickle fog was dissolving into shreds around me. The cold, white moon shone through the branches onto my bright plaid coat. I had to move on.

I remembered a bank only a few yards away, not far from the picnic area, where vines and underbrush tumbled over a shelf of rock. One of the children had crawled in it on the day of our outing. I took one cautious step, two, feeling my way in the darkness, until finally I found the niche and huddled there, concealed by the curtain of vines.

I wondered if Hannah had found help. Surely by now some kindly motorist had stopped. I shuddered to think what might happen if she met the other kind. The rock was cold and hard against my back, and there was barely room for my legs on the shelf. Cold and wet from the stream, they were beginning to cramp painfully. The constant throbbing in my arm had become a part of me. I cradled it against me, felt the hot swelling beneath my fingers. I listened for Essie's rugged breathing, her footsteps squishing on the hard ground. There was nothing. Maybe she *had* fallen for my trick and had continued in the other direction. In spite of my predicament, I smiled.

The chuckle came from below me, a part of the fog, gray and soft and cold as death. The evil of it reached out through the darkness, crept over me like a deadly viper waiting to strike.

"I know you're in there, Henrietta. I've been watching you, waiting for you to run yourself to the wall, and now you have! Obliging of you. Now there's no place left to run!" Her laugh turned to a cough, racking her body. "Will you come out now, or die in there like a snail on a rock?"

I eased my numb legs over the sharp edge of the rock and slid to the ground, my legs giving way beneath me. I could see her dim shape in the darkness and knew she must be as cold and wet as I was. Was the woman made of iron? Surely she must be exhausted!

Yet her madness had sustained her. She drew her strength from it.

Again she chuckled, louder, boastfully flinging her triumph in my face, wringing the last drop of satisfaction from it. "Guess you wish you'd stayed in the city now, don't you? Funny how you and your mother made the same mistakes."

I sat very still on the ground, sensing that any movement might provoke her. "Why *did* she come back, Essie?"

"What do you care? You're going to die anyway." She coughed again, drew her soggy coat around her.

"I can't understand how you managed to get away with killing all those people," I said, hoping to appeal to her ego. "Why did the police never suspect you?"

There was almost a swagger in her stance. "They had no reason. Even your mother didn't suspect me— until it was too late!"

"Why did she think it was Seth?" I asked.

She crept nearer. I thought she was going to kill me then, but instead she hesitated. Then she started to talk. She couldn't refuse an opportunity to gloat! "Maggie found that snapshot in the attic," she said. "She had moved into the main house that fall and had gone up there to store some things. I had hidden it in an old album; I thought it would be safe. She had no business poking in things that didn't concern her!"

I shivered. "And she thought Seth had put it there?"

Essie paced around me as if she were deciding from which angle to shoot. "She wasn't sure, but it frightened her, frightened her so much that she ran away. And she took the picture with her. Seth took that photograph, you see, and Maggie remembered that. He took it one Sunday afternoon. They had been playing dodge ball on the lawn after dinner, acting like children!"

She snorted. "They did that a lot, played games and acted silly like they didn't have anything better to do!" She thrust her face into mine. "Of course, that wasn't the only reason Maggie Grey left here!"

"She told you she was pregnant?"

"Oh, my, yes! She told me all about it. They were in love, she said. Love! She was sure he would come back!"

I was certain she could hear my heart beating. "And did he?"

"You don't see him, do you?" Essie threw back her head and laughed. "Of course he didn't come back! Why should he?"

"Who was my father, Essie?" I hoped she wouldn't hear the pleading in my voice.

Essie stepped away from me. Clutching the gun with both hands, she aimed it steadily at my chest. She's going to shoot me now, I thought. I'm going to die, never knowing . . .

"Your father? That's right, you wouldn't know, would you?" The words oozed from her, mockingly. "Your *father* was a stranger passing through, some reporter from an Atlanta paper here to cover all the excitement that summer. I can't even remember his name. 'My Cavalier,' she called him!" Her laughter brought on a spell of coughing, but the gun never wavered. "Some cavalier! He got what he wanted and left her holding the bag, or in her case, the baby! That was you, of course."

If the circumstances had been different I would have thanked her. Morgan was not my brother! I was free to love him now, now that it was too late.

I tried to keep from trembling, to speak in a steady voice. I had to keep her talking. "Do you think he ever knew?" I asked. "Did he ever try to find her?"

"What does it matter now? Oh, she waited around a while, stalked the phone, the mailbox. It was pathetic! Then, before I knew it, she was gone." Essie's voice grew stronger, more indignant. "Her father turned her out, and who could blame him? Several months later she wrote me from the city. Said she'd seen Seth there, which wasn't too surprising, since he was in college there, staying with a relative. It scared her out of her wits, poor, stupid woman! She thought Seth was stalking her, thought he knew she suspected him. Of course, she didn't tell me all this until she came back to Raven Rock. That's when I learned she had found that snapshot. I had posed the group, had planned it, but she didn't remember that!"

"So she came back to confide in you—Seth's mother—because she cared about you, because you were her friend!" I couldn't keep the fury out of my voice. "She could have gone straight to the police, but she didn't. She went to you."

"She didn't have enough evidence to go to the police. She would have made a fool of herself. They would never have believed her." Her voice was husky. "Now get up, Henrietta, very slowly, and start walking toward the lake. You've wasted enough time."

I stumbled to my feet. "They'll know you killed me, Essie. Hannah has probably told them what happened by now. What good will it do to kill me?"

"Hannah?" Her voice was puzzled. "Oh, the child! I doubt if she got very far. I'll deal with her later." I had shaken her confidence. The gun trembled in her hand.

"If the police don't get you, my mother will," I said, using my last, desperate tactic. "You chose the wrong place to murder me, Essie. Her spirit is here. I've felt it from the first." I looked beyond her to the falls, flung out my arm to include the swirling vapor curling around us. "Can't you feel it? The nearness of her? She's all around us, Essie. She could reach out and touch you."

"You're lying!" she screamed. "You're trying to trick me."

"You betrayed her," I continued. "You kept her from me. She'll never let you go."

"No!" Even in the darkness I could see the wildness in her eyes. In that moment she buckled, as if someone had grabbed her from behind. Perhaps she stumbled, or imagined in her fear that my mother was indeed present. But there was no one there, only the cool caress of the gray fog and the thunder of the falls.

In the panic of that moment, I ran, forgetting my coldness, my soggy, clinging clothing, the pain in my wrist. I ran toward the cabin and the beautiful yellow rays of bobbing lights—flashlights with people behind them coming to meet me in the dark!

"Henri! Watch out, behind you!" It was Morgan's voice. The terror in it froze me where I stood. In the glare of the flashlights, Essie stood a few yards below us, the gun at arm's length. "I'll kill you! I'll kill you all!" Her voice was choked with desperation. The hand that held the gun wavered and was still.

"No! Mother!" Seth stepped out in front of me, just as someone jerked me to the ground and threw himself on top of me, someone who smelled of woodsmoke and printer's ink.

"Son, you don't understand. I did it for you, all for you." I heard Essie's voice, old and quaking and soft with love, and the sharp report of the revolver like a cannon in my ears. Morgan cradled me to him, pressed my head into his shoulder, but not before I saw Essie slump to the ground, dead from her own gun.

Thirty-four

"Hannah?" I struggled against the drowsy comfort that overtook me in the security of Morgan's arms. "We have to find Hannah!"

"Hannah's fine." He stroked my matted hair. "She's at home now with her parents, and you're going home, too." I felt myself being lifted, carried in his arms, and that was the last thing I remembered until I woke the next day in a strange bedroom.

Alice Lawrence smiled when I opened my eyes. "Good afternoon! Which will it be first, a hot bath or some hot food?"

I groaned. I ached all over. Then I shuddered, remembering the events of the night before. "Was it real, Alice? Did Essie really . . . ?"

She nodded. "It's over now, Henri. It's best that she's gone." She touched me lightly on the forehead. "Morgan's waiting to see you, but I told him you'd probably want to get cleaned up first."

I looked at my mud-streaked arms crisscrossed with scratches, noticed the clean, white bandage on my wrist.

"You were exhausted when they brought you here last night," she explained. "After Chip dressed your wrist, I just slipped you into one of my gowns and let you sleep."

I grimaced at the thought of my mud-encrusted hair. "First the bath, I think, then the food!"

I sipped the hot, nutritious soup, feeling my body come alive. It was good to be wearing clean clothes again, my own clothes that Morgan had brought over from Honeysuckle House. He sat across from me as I ate, grinning with every bite, as if I were doing something marvelous. I couldn't take my eyes off him.

"Morgan Lawrence, I love you," I said, "and I hope you still feel the same about me, because I plan to spend the rest of my life with you."

The look in his eyes caused a pleasant, warm sensation in the pit of my stomach.

"If this is a proposal, I accept." He leaned over and kissed me lightly on the lips. "But isn't this a sudden change of tune? Whatever happened to your views on incest?" His voice feigned astonishment. "And what will the neighbors say?"

"My father was a reporter from Atlanta," I said, ignoring his teasing gaze. "Apparently a *roving* reporter!"

He nodded. "When did you find out? Did Dad tell you?"

"No, Essie did last night at the lake. If she hadn't been so willing to talk, to humiliate me, I probably wouldn't be here now." I forced a spoonful of soup past the lump in my throat. "It was almost worth it to find out the truth."

Morgan reached for my hand. "Dad could have told you that, Henri. We talked about it last night."

"About my father? Does he know who he is? Do you? Essie said she couldn't remember his name." I gripped his fingers until he drew them gently away.

"Hey, wait a minute! I don't know any more than you do. Dad will tell you about it." Morgan smiled. "Right now, let's take one thing at a time. Isn't it enough for now that we're here together and that you and Hannah are safe?"

"I'm so glad you found Hannah," I said. "If she hadn't brought help in time . . ."

He shook his head. "We didn't find Hannah, someone else did. A waitress from an all-night diner said that Hannah stepped out and tried to wave her down as she was driving to work. The waitress wasn't going to stop," Morgan went on, "until she saw it was a child. Hannah told her such a wild tale she took her straight to the police." He poured me another cup of tea. "But by then we had already started to the cabin."

I paused with my spoon in mid-air. "But how? How did you know?"

"After I left you at the cottage last night, I delivered Alice's cake to Essie. Then I stopped by *The Register* office to write my editorial. I don't know why, but while I was there I started thinking about what you had said."

I frowned. "About what?"

"About that letter you said your mother wrote, the one Miss Carrie saw. The more I thought about it, the more it worried me. I had the strangest feeling that something was not right. I thought maybe Seth had taken the letter, so I went over to the jail." He reached for a sandwich, turned it over in his hands. "Seth denied seeing the letter, but he acted as if he were holding something back. I knew he wasn't telling us all he knew." He sighed. "Anyway, I was there when Hannah's mother called about her being lost. It never occurred to me that she might have gone all the way to the cabin! The police seemed to think she might

213

have gotten lost in the wooded area behind her house, and I volunteered to help them. Of course, we found nothing," he added. "It was late when I got back to the station, and I was afraid Alice might be worried so I called to tell her about Hannah."

"Oh, I see, and Essie had told Alice." Our hands met across the table. Gently he traced the outline of my fingers.

"That's right. That's when I knew something was wrong. Alice said that you had planned on looking for Hannah at the cabin, but that Essie had called later and told her you decided to let the police handle it. It didn't ring true. I know how you feel about Hannah, and the officer on duty said you hadn't called there. We called you at Honeysuckle House, and no one was there. When we telephoned Essie's, the line was busy. Lieutenant Griswold and I drove there and woke the roomers. We found the receiver off the hook and Essie gone."

"But Hannah? When did she get back?"

"As we were leaving Essie's, we heard the news over the police radio that she had been returned," he said. "And when Seth heard what his mother had done, he volunteered to come with us." He enfolded my hand in his. "Henri, you don't know how hard I prayed that we would get there in time!"

I squeezed back the tears, wondering if I would ever erase the nightmare from my mind.

"Henri?" It was Alice, an anxious look on her face. "It's Seth. Do you think you're up to seeing him? He says he wants to talk with you." She shrugged. "I didn't know what to tell him."

I looked at Morgan, and he smiled. "Yes, of course I'll see him," I said.

Seth looked older, strained. Yet there was another quality about him, an ease that had not been there before. Seth had been released.

"Henrietta." He stood beside me, refusing the chair that was offered. "I had to see you, to tell you how sorry I am for allowing this to happen." His face twisted.

"Seth," I began, "please don't."

"Yes," he insisted. "I allowed it. I suspected something was wrong when I heard of that snapshot turning up at the cottage." He turned to Morgan. "You see, I *saw* Miss Carrie give Mother that picture! I was out of town when the kitten was killed, but I just couldn't believe she was responsible for that." He was silent for a minute, his head bowed. "But the night Pat was attacked, she came in late. I heard her, saw her wet shoes on the back porch. Of course, the next morning she denied ever going out." He sighed. "That's when I knew. I was afraid to let her out of my sight! I knew she needed help, but, oh God, what do you do when something like this happens to your own mother? Nobody would have believed me! I couldn't believe it myself. Henri, I never imagined she would go this far! I had no idea she would try to kill you!"

Morgan stood behind him, touched his shoulder. "So you went to jail for her."

He shuddered. "Oh, I was there in Henri's room all right, but not for the reason they thought. I woke up, you see, and found Mother gone. I was afraid for Henri, afraid she might try to frighten her, even harm her. So I let myself in with our key. We have a key, you know. That's how Mother got in when she did. I was going to try to stop her before she got to Henri. The policeman must have been dozing. I didn't see him; he didn't see me." He shrugged. "Anyway, I

215

could see that Mother wasn't there. I was leaving when Henri woke and heard me." He smiled. "I almost made it! Later I found out Mother had been working on her quilt in the laundry room. I didn't see the light under the door."

"Seth, do you remember Maggie Grey?" I realized he had no way of knowing what had happened to my mother. No one knew but me.

He smiled. "Of course, I do. Maggie was a friend of mine. She and her roommates asked me over for hamburgers sometimes." There was a boyish quality in his voice. "I was different as a teenager, lonely. Mother didn't like . . . well, she had funny ideas. They saw that, I think, Maggie and her friends. They were kind to me."

"Do you remember seeing her in the city?" I asked. "After she left Raven Rock?"

He thought for a minute. "Yes, as a matter of fact, I did. I saw her on the street one day, called to her, but she didn't answer. At the time I thought she didn't hear me. But something happened after that that I never understood. I happened to go into the bakery where she was working. I know she recognized me; I called her by name. She acted strange, ran into the back like she didn't want to be seen.

"She was pregnant, you know," he went on. "Even I could see that. Maybe she was ashamed, but it didn't matter to me! I was just glad to see her. Everyone was worried about her. No one in Raven Rock knew where she went."

"Did you tell anyone you saw her?" I asked.

He shook his head. "No. I could see she didn't want anyone to know, didn't want any more to do with us. Oh, I called her a few times, or tried to. Usually she hung up on me. The last time I called her, she seemed frightened, told me to leave her alone. I didn't bother her anymore after that." He looked at me. "She was in that snapshot, wasn't she? The one the police were asking about. I took that picture, you know. I remember the day. Everyone was in a playful mood that afternoon. Mother thought we should get a picture. And most of those women were murdered." His face turned white. "The Chuckler! But he, they say he's dead. *He* killed all those women! Surely they don't think . . ."

I suffered for him. I didn't want to be the one to tell him.

"I have to know, Henri. I'm sorry. Please, please! What happened to Maggie Grey? What do all those women have to do with my mother?" Seth's voice was strained. "The police have been searching the house all morning, asking questions."

"Maggie Grey was my mother, Seth. She left me with the Merediths as a baby and came back to Raven Rock to talk with your mother." I told him about her suspicions after finding the photograph, her fear upon seeing him in the city.

"She's dead, Seth. Maggie is dead. Your mother killed her that night at the lake. Her body is buried there near the falls. Essie killed her like she killed the others, Nell Gordon, Loretta Eddington, all of them."

He sank into the chair, his eyes glazed. "I don't believe you!"

"Henri, are you sure?" Morgan asked. "How can you be certain?"

"Because she told me!" I cried. "She was insane! Essie meant to bury me there, too. The family graveyard, she called it."

"Why are you doing this to me?" Seth asked. "Why are you saying these things?"

"Because it's true, Seth," I said. And I could tell by his eyes he knew it, too.

"I suppose they'll find some evidence. The police will reopen the case now. It will all come out." He sighed. "All these years," he said, "all these years I've lived with her and loved her."

"And she loved you," I said. "Your mother wasn't responsible for what she did. She was sick, Seth. Try to remember that."

"Where will he go?" I asked Morgan after Seth had left. "What will he do now?"

"Far away from here, I hope," he answered. "Maybe he can start over somewhere else. There's still time."

But there would be no time for Essie's victims: Maggie and Nell, dedicated teachers, the young widow Loretta Eddington, or the pretty teenager, Wilma Lou Tatum, who was just beginning to live. For them, time had run out.

Thirty-five

After Morgan went back to the office, I spent the remainder of the afternoon giving an account of the previous night to the police. They had questioned the roomers, as well as others who remembered the Chuckler murders. They also turned up a mask and other evidence among Essie's belongings. My statement and Hannah's verification came as no surprise, I found.

"From what we've learned so far, I'm almost certain Essie was telling you the truth," Lieutenant Griswold said. "However, we do have to take into consideration the fact that she was unbalanced. She might have identified so closely with the Chuckler that she actually believed she had done it."

"There's one way to find out, Lieutenant," I said. "My mother's grave."

"Yes," he agreed. "If her body is where Essie said it was, there should be no doubt about it." He looked away. "We talked with the Whitaker child this morning. She told us where Essie said your mother was buried. We have some men out there now."

"You'll let me know when . . . . if you find anything?"

He nodded, glancing out the window. "It's getting late, though, too dark to see. It might take a few days." I could see he was eager to leave. "Well, I see you have company coming, so I'll be getting along."

Company! Could it possibly be . . . ? Maybe Dr. Lawrence had gotten in touch with the man who was my father. I immediately ran to the window, but it was only Joyce and Dan. As glad as I was to see them, it was difficult to conceal my disappointment. My relief at finding out who *wasn't* my father had diminished the importance of his identity, yet curiosity gnawed at me.

I only nibbled at the delicious meal Alice prepared for dinner that night. Dr. Lawrence had come home tired and concerned over one of his elderly patients and said little during the meal. He seemed reluctant to discuss the subject of my father, and I hesitated to bring it up.

He watched me with a worried frown as we cleared away the dishes. Finally he pushed back his chair. "Morgan tells me you want to hear about your father," he said, leading the way into the den. He smiled briefly. "I understand you were concerned that I might be the one."

I sat next to him on the sofa while Morgan added wood to the fire. "Essie told me it was a reporter who was here covering the murders that summer," I said. "I guess that lets you off the hook." I wanted to apologize for the rude way I had treated him, but could think of no gracious way to do it.

The doctor's voice was gentle. "I was your mother's doctor as well as her friend, Henrietta, but I wasn't her lover."

Morgan grinned. "Thank heaven for that!"

"Maggie came to me when she first suspected she was pregnant," his father continued. "Of course, there was nothing I could do, nor would she have asked it. As far as I know, Essie and I were the only ones here who knew Maggie was expecting a child."

"But what about my father?" I asked. "Didn't he . . . ?"

Dr. Lawrence glanced at his wife, as if searching for an answer. "Are you sure you want to hear this, Henri?"

I nodded. I had come this far, and I knew I would never have any peace until I learned the answers.

"He never answered her letters, never returned her calls. I heard later that he'd been on a brief assignment out of the country, but even on his return he made no attempt to get in touch with Maggie." He shook his head sadly. "I'm sorry, Henri. There's not much more I can tell you, except that his name was Dixon Cavanaugh, and your mother loved him very much."

I had thought I had no tears left, but I cried for my mother as much in rage as in pity. And if Dixon Cavanaugh had walked into the room at that moment, I think I would have clawed him to shreds.

"Here, Henri, sip this slowly." Alice held out a snifter of brandy. "I'm so sorry you had to hear all this!"

I smiled. "At least I won't have to wonder anymore." The brandy went down like amber fire, but it warmed and relaxed me. Like someone in a dream, I watched the firelight play on the glass. "You haven't told me everything, have you?" I looked into the doctor's troubled eyes.

He stood and placed both hands on the mantel, leaning on it for support. "Dixon Cavanaugh was a good-looking fellow," he began. "Tall, sandy-haired, charmed all the ladies. Everyone called him Cav, except for Maggie. She liked to tease him about being her Cavalier.''

With a jab of the poker, he shattered a smoldering log as if it were my long-absent father. "Cav could have dated any girl in town," he continued, "but he only had eyes for Maggie. I think she fell in love with him from the start.''

The doctor poured a glass of brandy and stood with the drink in both hands. "Cavanaugh was attracted to Maggie in his way, Henrietta. Maybe he even thought he loved her, but Maggie had no money, no social connections. I heard later that he'd married a girl from Atlanta, a girl from a socially prominent and wealthy family. They set him up with his own newspaper, I believe.''

"I hope I never meet him," I said through clenched teeth, "or you'll have your work cut out for you. He'll need intensive care for at least a year!''

"Dixon Cavanaugh is dead, Henri," Dr. Lawrence said softly. "I read where he was killed in a plane crash several years ago.''

Morgan turned as if to comfort me, but I only shrugged. I felt nothing but emptiness and relief. The doctor looked so tired and sad, I went over and kissed him lightly on the cheek. "How long have you known who I was?" I asked.

It was good to see him laugh. "Well, I wasn't sure until Morgan told me, but I had a good idea. Oddly enough, it was Clayton Smith who first noticed your resemblance to Maggie. He mentioned it to me when he first met you.''

"Clayton Smith? You mean Mr. Smith who owns *The Register*? How did he know my mother?''

"He was here covering the murders for the Raleigh paper," Morgan's father told me. "In fact, for a while

222

I think he was interested in Maggie, too, but once Cavanaugh started seeing her, he dropped out of the picture."

"Pity," I said, "he seems like a nice man. But you know, for a while I thought our Mr. Smith might be the one causing all the trouble. He always looked at me so strangely, and the day of the bike hike I caught a glimpse of someone following Hannah and me—someone in khaki pants." I grinned. "And there he was, our Mr. Smith, in khaki pants!"

Alice's eyes widened. "Did you ever find out who it was?"

"Probably Essie. I think she followed me to the lake hoping to get me alone, but I was always with Hannah or the others. That was the night she called." I shivered, remembering.

Morgan stood to stretch. "Well, I wish someone had confided in me." He looked from his father to me. "You and Clayton guessed that Henri was Maggie's daughter; Henri thought you were her father, and I didn't know what to think . . . what a mess! And look how much time we've wasted."

"But we'll make up for it," I promised.

They found my mother's body a few days later at Raven Rock Lake. It was buried near the falls as Essie had said it would be. There wasn't much left to identify the pitiful remains of Maggie Grey, but the dental records and the ring she wore proved beyond a doubt that I had found my mother at last. We buried her next to her father in the small country cemetery at Shannon.

My grandmother came to stay with me in Honeysuckle House until I could make other arrangements. Morgan and I drove to Shannon to bring her back, and his father dropped by soon after we arrived. I was glad they were with me when Lieutenant Griswold came by to tell me they had found my mother's body. My grandmother clung to me as she cried, but I had no tears left for Maggie Grey. Both of us were relieved that it was over, but the shadow of her death would stay with us.

"I suppose this leaves no doubt that Essie was the Chuckler?" Morgan asked the detective.

The lieutenant's face was solemn. The strain of the past few days showed around his eyes. "Yes, it was Essie, and, if it hadn't been for Miss Meredith here, we might never have found out."

"What about the man they convicted?" I asked. "Didn't that little girl identify him?"

"Yes, and he did attack the child, but he didn't kill the others. Essie just used him. It happened at a convenient time, so she hid incriminating evidence in the old gin where he'd been sleeping. He was another victim in a way, although he did deserve to be punished for his own crime."

"That's right," Dr. Lawrence agreed. "I remember how he denied the murders at the trial. I wondered then if he was guilty of killing those women."

Morgan shook his head. "Essie! It's still hard to believe there was that side to her. Do you know why she did it? Was there a reason for her to hate these women so?"

"We've found out a lot about Essie Honeycutt in the last day or so," Lieutenant Griswold said. "Now people remember things they never thought of before. I don't think she really hated her victims. She thought they threatened her relationship with her son. Essie never intended to let Seth go."

"But most of them were much older than Seth!" I said. "How could she possibly think they were interested in him?"

"There's something most of you don't know about Essie," the detective said. "Or perhaps you've forgotten. Essie's husband left her after they had been married only a few years. That may have been the beginning of her problem. From what I've learned, things we've found that she'd written, Essie considered sexual relations vile. Her own marriage was a mockery, therefore all man-woman relationships were wrong. She was consumed by her desire to protect her son. All females, especially the younger ones who paid him any attention, were singled out as a threat to his purity."

I shivered. "And my mother and her roommate Nell were kind to him. Joyce, too, I'm sure, but Joyce married Dan, and that let her off."

"One of the roomers told me that Nell taught Seth to play chess. She always called him her 'buddy,' and once in a while she would playfully kiss him on the cheek." The lieutenant frowned. "She meant it in a sisterly way, but Essie didn't take it like that."

"What about the other woman, the one who ran a dress shop?" Morgan asked.

"From what I hear, Loretta Eddington was a flirt. She flirted with any male, from nine to ninety," the detective explained. "Seth helped her in the store sometimes on weekends, and he was planning on taking a summer job there as a stock boy." He paused. "Seth dated the Tatum girl a few times, and I think they were still friends, but Wilma Lou was planning to marry another man. Unfortunately for her, Essie didn't know that."

"There was another woman, one who got away," the doctor remembered. "She was a happily married woman with a family."

"Oh, yes!" The officer smiled. He seemed relaxed for the first time since I'd met him. "We wondered about that too. But Seth babysat for the Taylors, cut the grass, things like that. He was lonely, I suppose. He liked being around them. Sometimes they invited him over for cookouts, and I think he and Mrs. Taylor played tennis together a few times." He shrugged. "I guess Essie thought it was too much of a good thing."

"And she had Seth take that picture of them all together," I reminded them. "She must have planned it all along."

"It's funny," Morgan said, "but I always had the idea that Essie liked people, really liked them."

"I think she did, or the normal part of her did," Lieutenant Griswold told him. "I expect she liked you, Miss Meredith, and she was probably fond of your mother, until in her unbalanced mind you became an insurmountable problem."

Morgan shook his head. "Poor Seth! He should have left here years ago. He never had a chance for a normal life."

"This is mere speculation," the lieutenant said, "but I think Essie planned on moving back into Honeysuckle House once she got rid of you, Miss Meredith. I think that's why she changed her mind about having it renovated. She was old; she was tired; she had worked hard all her life taking care of other people. She wanted to go back to a place where she had been happy, just she and Seth, the way it once had been."

"Are you sorry, Henrietta?" Morgan asked me later. "Are you sorry you found out about your past?"

His father and the detective had left earlier, and my grandmother rested upstairs. I pulled his face down for a kiss. "How could I be sorry? I found you, didn't I? I found Grandmother." The small living room of Honeysuckle House was strangely dark and quiet, and I switched on a lamp to banish the gloom.

"I had to find out where I came from, and now I know," I said. "It's like finishing the last chapter of a book. You remember it, but you put it aside. It's over."

"Still," he began, "I wish things could have worked out better about your parents."

"The Merediths were my real parents," I reminded him. "They were the ones who loved me and raised me, and they'll always be Mom and Dad to me."

Outside a cold wind whipped branches about, but I was warm and safe in Morgan's arms.

"What's that cologne you're wearing?" he whispered into my neck. "Hmmm, reminds me of summer flowers . . ."

I smiled as he sniffed the air. "Honeysuckle, that's it!" Morgan nibbled my face, my neck, searching for the scent. "Funny how it comes and goes. It was strong for a while, and now it's gone."

And probably for good, I thought. But I liked being nibbled, so I didn't tell him I wasn't wearing cologne. That would be my secret. Maggie's and mine.